# THE IN THE MARSH

### By

### Steven A. McKay

**Copyright © 2021**
No part of this book may be reproduced,
in whole or in part, without prior written
permission
from the copyright holder.

*Dedicated to Mrs Boodell and the
children of Year 5 at St Edmund's Primary.
Just wait until you're all a bit older
before you read it!*

# CHAPTER ONE

**Yorkshire, England
October, AD 1330**

"Open up, in the name of King Edward!"

There was a terrific hammering at the door, loud enough to wake the dead which, as fate would have it, was exactly how Thomas Brewer felt as he came to.

Thomas had downed a fair amount of ale at the nearby tavern that night, stumbled home in a good mood after winning money from some other drinkers in a game of dice, and gone to sleep in an even better humour after he'd made his wife perform what he called 'her marital duties'.

He wasn't a popular man, Thomas Brewer, either in the alehouse or at home. His children had grown up and been glad to leave his stifling, controlling presence, for he was a man who believed youngsters needed regular beatings to keep them in line. Whether they'd done anything 'wicked' or not.

The thumping at the door started again and Thomas retched, his head pounding from the earlier alcohol consumption. "Bugger off!" he bellowed, rubbing his eyes and turning to see his wife staring at him fearfully in the moonlight that was spilling through a gap in the shutters.

"Why's the bailiff here?" she asked him quietly. "It's the middle of the night."

"How should I know?" Thomas spat, holding his head in his hands as the pounding continued.

"Open up," their visitor shouted. "Or I'll break the door down."

Although the Brewers lived in the village of Penyston, their house was set about half a mile away from the centre. Despite the noise the bailiff was making, it was unlikely any of the local gossips would be coming to find out what was happening. Even Thomas knew he wasn't well-liked.

This crossed Thomas's drink-addled mind and, enraged by his rude awakening, he pushed himself up and lifted the heavy wooden cudgel which he always kept beside his bed.

"Last chance," the man outside shouted, ceasing his knocking for a moment at least. "Open the door, Brewer, or it'll go badly for you."

There was a jug of ale on the table which he and his wife sat at for their meals and, as he headed towards the door, Thomas lifted the jug and without bothering to find a cup, lifted it to his lips and swallowed a long draught.

"I'm coming," he called, upending the jug into his mouth again then stepping across to the door. He closed his eyes and pressed his back against the wall, wishing the ale would work its magic upon him as soon as possible and take away that infernal headache. "What d'you want anyway?" he called.

"You owe the king money, Brewer," replied the bailiff. "You've had enough time to pay your fines and shown no willingness to do so. I know you were at the alehouse earlier, and I know you won money, so I'm here to collect what you owe."

"At this hour?" Thomas shouted incredulously. "Couldn't you have waited until it was light? Are you mad?"

"Maybe I am," the man outside laughed menacingly. "Now, open up, you useless bloody cretin, before—"

Absolutely livid at the bailiff's insult, and finally feeling the warmth of the ale he'd just downed spreading empoweringly through his body, Thomas quickly drew back the heavy bolt on the door and charged outside. He saw a tall figure in the darkness and swung his cudgel at it, aiming for the head. He wasn't trying to warn the man off – Thomas wanted to really teach this bailiff a lesson he wouldn't forget.

His swing was wild, however, and it whistled through thin air as its target ducked out of the way, and then, somehow, Thomas found himself on the ground, staring up at the moon.

He tried to speak, to ask what was happening, but he felt something fill his mouth and then, horrified, he realised it wasn't vomit he was tasting. It was blood.

The moonlight glittered off the longsword in the bailiff's hand and Thomas, utterly astonished, saw the blood dripping from the blade. His blood. He felt the wound now, deep, very deep, in his guts, and he saw his attacker's face.

Coughing blood out of his mouth, Thomas managed to gasp, "Why, bailiff?" before a boot smashed into his head and that terrible longsword plunged into his body again, and again, until Thomas lay outside his own home, unmoving, blood pooling around him.

The hooded killer looked inside the house, sword raised, but Thomas's wife hadn't moved out of the bed. She was watching everything, clearly too terrified to get up, or even to cry out.

The figure stepped inside the low, single-roomed building, and walked across to the bed, face hidden by the shadows and the hood. He saw the coin purse Thomas had earlier dropped onto the table beside the ale jug and lifted it.

"This belongs to the king," he said in a gruff although shaky voice, then turned and walked out of the house, stepping over the body he'd left at the threshold and disappearing into the night.

At last, Thomas Brewer's wife found her voice, and, despite the distance to Penyston, half the village was woken by the screams that filled the moonlit countryside that cold October night.

# CHAPTER TWO

"Fresh fish, get your fresh fish! Bailiff! What about you?" The merchant held up a brown trout, glistening in the pale, morning sunlight, but his prospective customer shook his head. "What about a nice eel, then?"

"Not today," John replied, smiling at the man's continued efforts to sell his wares. "I'm busy."

The fishmonger wasn't listening, his interest gone as he realised he wouldn't make any money from the bailiff. Instead, he turned his attention to an elderly woman who was poking about amongst the crate of trout. "Good choice, my lady," he said effusively. "Look at the size of that. Keep you going for a while that will, and it'll taste like heaven if I'm any judge."

The bailiff, an enormous, bearded man known as Little John, walked on, eyes moving across the bustling market, searching for one man in particular. John was employed by the sheriff as a roving debt-collector, not tied to a single town or village but travelling across Yorkshire and Nottinghamshire when required, collecting fines from debtors who were considered more dangerous than most. Men and women who'd refused to pay their dues to the crown and threatened, or even assaulted, the local bailiffs when they'd gone to collect what was owed.

John was well known across the entire country thanks to his time as a member of Robin Hood's fabled outlaw band. It was a brave, stupid, or very drunk criminal who tried to take him on in a fight. The sheriff, Sir Henry de Faucumberg, understood all this, which was why he employed John in this capacity and had asked him to collect an unpaid fine from the butcher here in Darton.

The bailiff hoped to see the fellow hawking his wares at the market that day. He'd be unlikely to make a run for it if it meant leaving behind all his meat. Then again, this butcher wasn't known as the type to run from a fight…

"Mutton! Winter's just about on us, can't beat a nice bit of mutton in a broth at this time of year, eh?"

John headed for the voice, pushing between the men and women who'd travelled from far and wide for the market that day until, at last, he stood before a stall laden with cuts of raw meat.

The butcher was handing a damp sack to a man who paid with some small coins and wandered off with his prize, presumably to make the suggested broth. As the happy customer was swallowed up by the crowd, the butcher looked up, opening his mouth to address John. Recognition flared in his eyes and he gripped the wicked-looking cleaver in his hand more firmly.

Even people who'd never met the bailiff knew him. At over six and a half feet tall, with his bushy brown beard and soldierly bearing, there weren't many like him in the north of England.

"What d'you want?" the butcher growled.

"What you owe the king, Simon," replied Little John coolly.

"I already told those other bastard bailiffs," the butcher said through gritted teeth. "I ain't got it. There's no point—"

"I'm not here to argue with you," John told him, and he pushed back the heavy cloak he was wearing, revealing the sword at his waist. He raised his voice now, so any would-be customers could hear. "You were found guilty of selling rotten meat, Simon, and you were dragged through Woolley and put in the stocks for it. That meat killed a young boy, it was so rancid."

"They couldn't prove that," the butcher shouted angrily, waving his blade in the air. Already the villagers were moving back, away from the confrontation, but not too far that they would miss the excitement.

"It's just as well for you that they couldn't prove it," John spat. "Or you'd have had more to deal with than a time in the stocks and a fine. Which you still haven't paid."

"Is this all true, butcher?" someone shouted, safely hidden amongst the crowd.

"Aye, it's true," John said. "And he attacked the two bailiffs that came to collect the money from him last week."

Simon wasn't from this village, he'd just travelled there that day to sell his meats, so he had no friends there to back him up. That being said, John might have been well known and even well respected throughout Yorkshire, but he was still a lawman, and those were never popular among certain elements of the population.

The butcher was silent, weighing his options, and then he grinned. "I told you, I don't have the money. That fine was ridiculous, I'm just a hard working man, not some wealthy sort. You people always pick on the likes of me, instead of going after the rich churchmen and the like."

"Aye," a man in the crowd shouted. "That's true."

"Damn bailiffs," another cried. "If you made the rich pay their taxes you wouldn't have to bother us poor folk."

John turned and said to the people gathered to watch, "Did you not hear me? The butcher sold rancid meat in Woolley and it killed a lad! This isn't about rich against poor. It's about a useless sack of shit being punished for his crimes."

"Look out!"

Not all in the crowd were hostile towards him, and, the moment he heard the warning John was drawing his sword and spinning to face the butcher. Just as well, for the man had slipped around the side of his wagon and his cleaver was arcing through the air towards the bailiff. Without the villager's cry of alarm John would surely have been badly injured.

The two blades came together with a ringing clatter and the crowd shrank back, shouting fearfully, or even excitedly. Market day was always a pleasure in a sleepy village like this, but no-one had expected such fine entertainment that day!

The butcher was a strong man who knew how to wield his cleaver. He'd spent a lifetime slicing skin and sawing through bones, and he was well known in his own town as a brawler who enjoyed starting – and ending – fights in all the local alehouses.

Despite all this, John was a trained swordsman with a much longer reach and, when he parried the butcher's first attack, he stepped back, set his feet defensively and easily batted aside the next few blows.

Now Simon's face fell, for he knew he couldn't get close enough to stab the bailiff, and he also knew John could kill him if he wanted to. Fear replaced the murderous rage in his eyes as he remembered all the old stories about Robin Hood's men and the brutality they'd been renowned for.

Little John might be a lawman, but he was capable of extreme, deadly violence. There were enough stories and songs about him to back that up.

Desperation could make a man more dangerous, however, and, somehow – perhaps John was distracted by a movement in the crowd beside him – the butcher's cleaver caught the bailiff's arm. A bright-red, bloody line appeared on the white skin and John roared in pain.

Before Simon could decide what to do next, press his attack or, more probable, run for his life, John stepped forward and smashed the pommel of his sword into the butcher's mouth.

Simon staggered back almost comically, spitting out bloody teeth, and then he fell onto his knees and pitched forward onto the ground. He didn't move after that, and, for what felt like a long time, everyone just stared, from the butcher's prone form to that of the grimacing bailiff whose arm was bleeding heavily.

"Fetch clean water," a woman said to her son. "And linen." He ran off towards their house which wasn't far off, and she hurried to John's side. "That's a nasty wound," she said, examining it expertly. "But you already know that, I'm sure. Sit down, before you fall down like that idiot."

Despite his injury, John laughed and the sound seemed to take all the fear and alarm from the atmosphere. Others laughed, and chattered excitedly about what had just happened, while the lady knelt beside the bailiff and pushed aside his sleeve.

Her son returned quickly, and, when she used the water he'd brought to wash John's cut she nodded in satisfaction. "It's not as deep as I'd feared," she said.

"I had a feeling he might want a fight," John said. "So I wore leather bracers." He shook his sleeve and the leather armour fell out onto the ground, sliced cleanly in half. There were whistles and gasps from the crowd as they realised what would have happened had he not been wearing the bracers.

"That probably saved your life," said the woman, still washing away the blood before taking the linen her son handed her and using it to tightly bandage the wound. "Or at least your arm."

A middle-aged, balding man walked over to them, and he didn't look particularly happy.

"You might have told me what you were doing, bailiff," he said irritably. "All this might have been avoided."

John grinned up at him. He knew Arthur, headman of the village, and he knew the fellow would have only got in his way if he'd told him why he was there. "Not to worry," he told the headman. "No harm done."

"No harm? He's dead!"

The butcher groaned just then and pushed himself up on his arms before groaning again and sagging back onto the ground.

"No, he's just got a sore face and a few less teeth," the bailiff replied cheerily. "But he still owes the king a lot of money. Thank you, lady." He smiled at the woman who'd finished bandaging his arm and got back to his feet.

"Not much chance of you getting anything out of him," the headman grumbled. "Unless you can sell the teeth he spat out."

"Oh, I've got an idea how to get at least some of what Simon owes." John turned to his nurse and said, "Is your lad busy? I'm going to need some help."

# CHAPTER THREE

"So, you became a merchant for the rest of the day?" Will Scaflock laughed, gesturing towards the innkeeper to refill their drinks. "I wish I'd seen that."

"Aye," John said, sitting back and basking in the heat from the nearby hearth. "Me, sitting in a chair, holding my injured arm and drinking ale – purely to take the edge off the pain, of course. Haggling with the villagers while the boy helped them with the meat they bought."

"Did you actually make enough to cover the butcher's fine?" asked a man in a grey friar's robe.

"We did, Tuck." John said, grinning. "I sold the meat for much less than it was worth, just to get rid of it as fast as possible but, even so, made enough to cover Simon's fine *and* pay the lad for his help, with a little extra to thank his ma for bandaging me up."

The innkeeper bustled over to their table with a heavy jug and used it to top up the three mugs, receiving coins and hearty thanks in return.

"Did she put a poultice or anything on it?" Tuck asked more seriously. He'd often been the one to tend to their old outlaw gang's injuries, either physical or spiritual, when they'd been hiding out in the greenwood.

"Aye," John nodded, froth from the ale sprouting along his beard as he took another drink. "And Amber checked it all again when I got home today, don't worry." Mention of his wife made John smile. They'd been together for the best part of two decades but were as close as ever. She was never happy to see

John injured, of course, but trying to get him to settle down to a quiet life as a blacksmith, which he'd been in his youth, was a waste of time. A man like Little John needed some adventure in his days, and he certainly found that, often with Will and Tuck by his side.

Most of the chat in the alehouse recently had been about young King Edward, third of that name, and his recent daring *coup d'état* against his regent, Roger Mortimer. Although just seventeen, Edward had forcibly taken control of the country and imprisoned both Mortimer and his own mother, Isabella. The whole affair had been quite a sensation locally, for the arrests had taken place when Edward and his supporters used a secret passage to enter Nottingham Castle, a place John and his friends were very familiar with. Now, Mortimer was on his way under guard to the Tower of London, where he'd famously escaped from seven years before. Word was he wouldn't be so lucky this time, however, as the new king had wanted to hang his former regent immediately but been advised to give him a trial first.

It was a time of great uncertainty in England, and the people of Wakefield desperately hoped this new young king would prove to be a good ruler. These momentous events weren't the only thing causing excitement within the village, though.

"Aye, the thing had *no face*. I nearly shit myself in fright!"

The three companions all turned at the voice, which belonged to a man in his late twenties who was sitting with some of the other villagers at a table on the opposite side of the fire.

"'No face'?" Will demanded. "What are you talking about now, Farrier? You been eating those funny mushrooms again?"

The storyteller shook his head but wasn't offended by Will's comment, or the laughter it engendered. Hardly anyone in Wakefield knew the man's Christian name, but he was a farrier, and that's what everyone called him.

"No, Scarlet," retorted Farrier, using Will's own nickname, bestowed as a result of his famously short temper. "I was out walking near the marshes—"

"Thinking about the smith's daughter," one of his friends put in, drawing more good-natured laughter but no denial from the farrier.

"I was out walking," he continued. "You know that old ruined manor house in the east, towards Altofts? The one that has a moat around it? Well, I saw it there, and it wasn't my imagination."

"Saw what?" Tuck asked eagerly. He loved stories like this, told beside the fire on a cold night as the autumn wind blew brown and orange leaves from the trees outside.

"A ghostly figure," Farrier said seriously. "As big as you, John," he nodded at the bailiff. "In fact, bigger. It was going towards the old manor house which, as you know is just ruins these days. As it got to the doorway, it turned around and looked right at me and, I swear by all that's holy, Brother Tuck, it had no face."

The scene he was describing had a powerful effect on the people gathered in the alehouse for they were all familiar with the area he'd described. The thought of a ghostly apparition haunting the manor house didn't seem that incredible – it had long been rumoured to be cursed. Unearthly lights, strange noises, screams, even hidden treasure…All, and more, had been reported by folk passing by in the decades since it had been abandoned and begun its slow decay into the ruin it now was.

Will made a face, one that suggested he thought Farrier was mad, but neither John nor Tuck were so quick to dismiss the strange tale out of hand. For all his skill in battle and prodigious strength, John could be quite superstitious and Tuck, being a clergyman, knew demons were very real.

"What did you do?" Will demanded.

Farrier looked sheepish. "Ran for my life, obviously. What would you have done? Actually, don't answer that." He grinned, not bothered by his friends' good-natured ribbing at the admission he'd fled. "If anyone could start a fight with a ghost, it'd be you, Scarlet."

"He's right there," John agreed, grinning.

"Some of us are going to visit the place tomorrow night," Farrier told them. "Us," he gestured at his drinking companions, "and some of the other villagers. I'm not the only one that's seen an apparition in those marshes recently. You want to come, lads? Maybe we'll find the stash of loot the cursed nobleman's said to have hidden there."

Will shook his head. "Nah, I'm trimming my toe-nails tomorrow night. It'll probably be more exciting than stumbling about the marshes in the dark with a load of idiots."

"God's bollocks," John rumbled in horror. "I think I'd rather face Satan himself than see you cutting your toe-nails. I'll come, Farrier. What about you, Tuck?"

"Aye, me too. You might need a man of God with you." The friar smiled and supped his ale beatifically. "You sure you won't join us, Will?"

Scarlet sighed heavily and rolled his eyes. "Oh, all right then. I suppose you'll need someone to take care of you if you *do* see a ghost. Besides, I wouldn't want to miss out on any treasure you lot find!"

# CHAPTER FOUR

Farrier had been right when he said other villagers had seen strange things in the nearby marshes, and they were happy to share their stories as the party from Wakefield – fourteen men and women of all ages and a couple of rangy dogs – made their way to the east the following evening.

Some claimed, like Farrier, to have seen a tall, hooded figure without a face. Others told of hearing strange, mocking laughter from the derelict manor house. One man even claimed to have crossed paths with a walking corpse, pale and covered in blood, although that particular witness was known to exaggerate.

The tales were exciting and creepy and made the journey to the marshes much more interesting than it would usually be, especially since it was dark and cloudy, with no moon to light their way. For that they had to rely on lanterns and Tuck wondered if this was a sensible way to spend an evening. He wouldn't have missed it though, and as they neared their destination he shared an amused look with John, for Scarlet was strangely quiet. Subdued. Of course, no-one suggested he might have been frightened…

The manor house was a great dark shadow looming up out of the marshes, the waters of which glistened in the light of the lanterns. The chattering of the villagers subsided as they approached the brooding, centuried ruin and the eeriness of the setting subdued their earlier, almost giddy excitement.

"Look," a woman whispered, pointing a trembling finger towards the side of the manor house.

"What?" Tuck asked, squinting into the darkness.

"A light. There was a light!"

"In the house?"

"Aye! In the back, I think."

Everyone looked but, if there had been anything illuminating the interior of the building it was gone now. All appeared dark and silent within.

"What now?" Little John wondered.

"We wait and see if any devils appear," someone said, and, as if on cue, the villagers – who seemed to have some experience of such vigils – took out blankets and laid them on top of large stones to sit on in some degree of comfort. "With any luck the ghostly figure will appear and lead us to his buried treasure."

John turned to Tuck, frowning. "Is that it? We just sit, and wait?"

The friar shrugged.

"But it's bloody freezing," John protested. "I thought we were going into the ruins."

A dozen or so faces turned to stare up at him, incredulous and pale in the wan light.

"Are you mad?" someone demanded. "The place is haunted!"

"I know," John said incredulously. "That's why we're here."

"On you go then," Farrier told him. "We'll watch."

Even Tuck was sitting on one of the villagers' blankets by now and, when John turned to Will he was met with raised palms and a silent, protesting shake of the head.

John gazed around at them all, then at the eldritch ruins which appeared more sinister with every passing moment, and the prospect of wandering into them, alone, was not appealing.

"Move over then, Tuck," he grumbled, folding his great legs and nudging the friar over. "I guess we'll just wait and watch, and hope something happens."

They spent two or three hours there, looking and listening expectantly but, apart from a scream which Scarlet assured them was a fox, and a swooping dark shape with eyes that seemed luminous – a barn owl, surely – nothing happened to break the monotony. Eventually, with everyone being mindful of the fact they'd need to be up early the next day for their work, the party packed away their soggy blankets and returned to Wakefield.

"We'll be going again," Farrier said to Tuck, John and Will as they reached the village and prepared to go their separate ways, homewards. "Will you lads join us?"

Scarlet gave a short, disgusted laugh, while John and Tuck shook their heads and said, less rudely, that they would not.

"Unless you're going inside," John added thoughtfully. "I'd be interested to go in and see what the place is like."

"Why don't you just go during the day?" Scarlet demanded.

"That'd be no fun," John replied simply, and received another snort of laughter in reply.

"He's right," Farrier said. "But, on top of that, the old legends say the ghost's treasure can only be seen at night, glistening in the light of the moon. Or the stars, maybe." He clearly wasn't sure of the truth of the old stories himself.

Will raised an eyebrow and opened his mouth to make another sarcastic reply, but instead he just looked from Farrier to John and wandered homewards without another word.

"We'll see you again, then," Farrier said to John. "You'll come with us on our next visit?"

"Aye," John replied. "If I can. I'm not sure about hidden treasure, but I'd quite like to see what's inside those old walls."

# CHAPTER FIVE

Horbury was a quiet town, generally. The headman, bailiff, and most of the people who lived there were hard working and peaceful, but they didn't stand for criminals operating around their homes. Usually, such types would be run out of town.

Usually.

Henry Engayne was another matter, however. Henry was a thief, and everyone knew it, but he was clever enough to never be caught in the act, and he had family connections who were wealthy and thus powerful enough to make the authorities wary of arresting him. Without sufficient proof he'd ever done anything wrong Henry would simply be set free and his relatives would cause trouble for those responsible for charging him.

As a result of all this, Henry Engayne was a much maligned and feared figure in Horbury. No-one wanted to upset him, in case he burgled their house or business in the night so, although not a violent man, people tried to avoid him when possible.

Not everyone was afraid of him, however.

"Engayne, you little shit!"

The door of the alehouse burst open and the red-faced, hulking form of the blacksmith, Stephen, stormed inside, eyes fixed on the slightly built man at the table nearest the hearth.

"You robbed my takings during the night, didn't you?"

Henry frowned, a look of bemused innocence on his stubbled face. "I don't know what you're talking about," he said, looking at the barman as if butter wouldn't melt in his mouth. "I was asleep all night."

The blacksmith stormed across the room, ignoring the four or five other drinkers in the alehouse, and grabbed Henry by the collar.

"I know it was you, you bastard. One of my neighbours saw someone matching your description skulking about in the middle of the night when they got up to take a piss, and my workshop had been broken into when I got there this morning."

"I'll…" Henry tried to speak but choked as the smith squeezed his throat tighter. "I'll have you arrested for assaulting me," he finally managed to gasp out, and his words drew a laugh of disbelief from Stephen who finally let go of him and stepped back, shaking his head in despair.

He knew Henry could do what he threatened – it just seemed to be how things worked with him. The blacksmith couldn't prove Henry had robbed his workshop, but Stephen could prove he'd been assaulted. There were witnesses in the alehouse after all.

Stephen looked at the barman, and the drinkers who were all staring at the confrontation. The blacksmith didn't recognise one of the men and a thrill of fear ran down his spine as he thought for a moment the stranger might even be a lawman. He was beginning to regret coming here and laying hands on Henry Engayne, who, for his part, was watching Stephen with a look as sly as any fox.

"Everyone in this town knows what you are," the smith growled, pointing a shaking finger at Henry.

"You're a thief, and one of these days you'll steal from the wrong man, and get what's coming to you."

"Threatening me now?" Henry cried, turning to the other men in the alehouse, an injured look on his face. "You all heard that – the blacksmith's threatening me."

None of the others said a word in reply. They simply stared in disgust at Henry, for they did indeed know what he was like, and hated him for it. Everyone in Horbury suspected they'd been robbed themselves by him, or someone they knew had.

Only the stranger appeared less hostile – instead, he was stroking his bushy beard and watching things with great interest, but offered no words of support to either Stephen or Henry.

"You must know my daughter's been poorly lately," the blacksmith said, still furious but more in control of himself by now. "I've been saving to pay for a barber-surgeon to help her. That money you stole from me…" He shook his head and, with a last, enraged look at the barman, stormed out and was gone.

Only the crackling of the log on the fire filled the silence his departure left behind until, after a time, Henry smirked, rubbed his neck where the smith had choked him, and said, "Bring me another drink, Alfred. And draw one each for the other fine fellows here – I'm feeling generous today." With that, he pulled out a handful of coins from a purse at his belt and dropped them onto the table with a laugh.

Although they accepted his drinks, not one of the other men joined in with Henry's laughter or thanked him, but it didn't seem to bother him and, a few hours later, when it was dark, he left the now-busy alehouse and headed for home.

He was in a good mood but, as he entered the narrow street that led to his own house, Henry stopped, listening, and then looked back over his shoulder.

"Whassat?" he muttered. "'Oo's there?" The street seemed empty though, and he muttered nervously to himself for he thought he'd heard footsteps behind him. And, as he continued on, he heard them again, and once more spun around to see who was there.

This time he was not alone.

"Oh, hello," he said, recognising the big stranger who'd been in the alehouse earlier.

"Did you rob the blacksmith?" the man asked, his voice calm and level and betraying no evidence that he'd been supping ale for much of the day. Instead, he looked quite sober and, taking in his height and muscular build, Henry began to feel nervous.

"No," he replied indignantly. "Now bugger off. What's it to you anyway?" He turned and started walking towards his house again, a little more steadily now as this encounter had sobered him up somewhat.

"I'm a bailiff," the stranger said. "And I don't like seeing criminals like you getting away with their trans…" He paused, as if unsure of the word he was looking for, and then said, "Crimes," instead.

"I haven't *transgressed* against anyone," Henry spat, lip curled in disdain at the fellow's stupidity. "So, be on your way, oaf. I have powerful friends who'll see you lose your nice job."

Suddenly, Henry felt a thud against his back, and he fell forward, gasping. There was a second thump in the same place and now he dropped onto his knees, the strength in his legs gone in an instant.

He could tell something was very wrong, for the blows hadn't felt that powerful, yet he couldn't even attempt to rise as the stranger knelt behind him. There was a jerking motion and the leather thong that attached Henry's coin purse to his belt fell away.

"Here," he gasped, reaching back and pressing a hand against the spot where he'd been struck. "What are you doing?" He brought his palm around and saw, with horror, that it was sticky with blood.

A shutter was flung open in the house beside them, candlelight illuminating their forms dimly as a face peered out.

"'Ere," said the old woman that was peering at them. "What's going on?"

"I'm a bailiff," the stranger replied in a harsh, breathless tone. "Just collecting a fine from this criminal."

"Help me!" Henry whimpered, but his words did not have the desired effect for the woman simply slammed her shutters without another word, leaving the two men in near-total darkness again.

"Lawbreakers like you make me sick," growled the stranger, leaning down to gaze into Henry's tear-streaked, drawn face. "Life's hard enough without your kind of scum robbing folk." His hand shot out again, and this time Henry saw the glint of steel as the blade plunged into him. It was the last thing he ever saw.

# CHAPTER SIX

"So, what's the story with this ghost then?" Little John stared across the marshes at the ruined manor house, its moat thick with weeds and green, slimy water, and he shuddered.

Friar Tuck made the sign of the cross and mouthed a prayer, silently blessing the site which they'd come to see during the day. They had no plans to actually go into the old building, indeed, they weren't even sure there was a safe way to do so – not without getting utterly soaked, at least. Between them, the marsh and the moat seemed to be well on their way to claiming the entire structure.

"Ralph de Mandeville," the friar said in reply to John's question. "An earl, I believe, who had a channel cut from the River Calder all the way here to fill his moat. It didn't work quite as intended though and ended up making the land marshy. He wasn't a very nice man by all accounts."

"Why doesn't that surprise me?" John muttered sarcastically.

"He used to kidnap nobles and torture them until their relatives paid a ransom for their release. Even kidnapped a family member of the king, which resulted in him being found guilty of treason." Tuck shook his head sadly. "He really did a lot of nasty things to people, eventually resulting in his excommunication by the Abbot of York."

John's eyes widened. Excommunication was a terrible thing, a punishment reserved only for the most wicked of people. Or those deemed so by the

Church at least, which, admittedly, wasn't always a good way to judge a person's moral fibre…

"That's why he still haunts this place," the friar said. "He died – either by being shot in the head with an arrow, or by falling into a well somewhere on this property, the tales aren't clear." Tuck gestured vaguely towards the crumbling house, having no idea where any such well might be located.

John gave a low whistle. "Died while excommunicated, eh? Damned for all eternity, and no Christian burial!"

"Well," Tuck said. "That's not really clear either. Some say the Templars came to Ralph on his deathbed and carried his body away, later receiving absolution on his behalf and burying him on some consecrated ground belonging to their Order." He shrugged. "Who knows? Perhaps none of the story is true, and no such person as Ralph de Mandeville ever existed. He's supposed to have lived over a hundred years ago. Even if he did, I don't know how anyone can tell it's his ghost that haunts this place."

They watched as a carrion crow settled on one of the manor house's walls, pecking at something and cawing as if in greeting to some hidden companion, and then it took off clumsily before wheeling out of sight behind the trees to the rear of the building. Whether 'Ralph de Mandeville' was a real person or not, it didn't really matter – there were plenty of real noblemen around, even nowadays, doing horrible things to people. They were often untouchable thanks to their wealth and influence, so the idea that they'd be punished in the afterlife, by being doomed to haunt the scene of their crimes forever, was an appealing one to the folk of Wakefield and beyond.

"There's all sorts of stories told about the ghost," Tuck said. "Or so Farrier told me when I questioned him about it in the alehouse last night."

"Farrier seems very interested in all this," John noted.

Tuck nodded. "Some people love a good ghost story around this time of year, eh? Makes the dark nights that little bit creepier."

"They're bloody creepy enough," John said. "Without adding spirits and hauntings."

"Ralph, or whoever the ghost is," Tuck said, "apparently clanks his spurs at people he comes across in the night. And he wears a red cloak."

"Did I hear someone saying he has a headless dog as a companion?"

Tuck laughed shortly. "Aye, that's another of the legends. No doubt there's various tales about how the dog lost its head too."

"It *should* be ridiculous," John mused, taking out a leather ale-skin and helping himself to a drink as they stared at the old house. "But once night falls, that building – which just looks sad to me right now in the daytime – becomes a lot more sinister. It's easy to believe some dead earl haunts the empty rooms when only the moon is about to light the place."

They eyed the silent ruins, wondering what grim events the crumbling walls had played host to over the years, and why such an expensive house had simply been abandoned. It must have been a wonderful building when it was first erected.

"Should we try and get inside?" John asked, looking down at his friend with an almost playful look. "There's still a couple of hours of daylight left. You've got your cross to protect us; I've got my sword."

Tuck turned to stare uncertainly at him. "Just the two of us? Er, no," he shook his head and chuckled. "I'll leave it for now. No point disturbing whatever dark force is slumbering there, and I've no need for treasure. Why don't you ask Will to go with you?"

"Will?" John grinned. "He's even more frightened than you. Didn't you hear him the other night when we were here, muttering about ghosts and devils and witches and all sorts? There's no chance he'd go exploring with me. Come on, let's head back home, the house will still be there another day."

The pair turned and started the walk back to Wakefield, drawing their cloaks tighter about them as the wind picked up, blowing leaves all around them and making it feel much colder than it had before. Winter had come at last.

# CHAPTER SEVEN

Beatrice poured the small pot of milk into a wooden mug and warmed her hands over it, waiting for it to cool down. It was bitterly cold that evening, November being ushered in with the first flurry of snow since the previous February, and the old peasant lady was looking forward to a hot drink in front of the crackling fire. Her house was set a little apart from the others in the village of Nostell, but her neighbours often brought her supplies – such as the milk she'd just been heating, bread, and even meat – and she made them healing poultices and elixirs in return.

As a healer, Beatrice was a good one, somehow understanding better than most so-called barber-surgeons what a person needed to make them feel better.

Of course, a power like that, along with the cats that lived in an around her hovel, meant rumours of witchcraft had attached themselves to Beatrice over the years. No-one in Nostell really believed such stories, for they knew the woman, and knew she was not a witch. It was laughable really.

She sat on her stool and lifted the mug of milk, blowing on it to try and cool it faster. The smell of it filled the single-roomed dwelling and Beatrice gave thanks to God for the kindly farmer who'd brought it to her, asking only for her to pray for his cows' continued health.

At last, she was able to sip the milk, instantly feeling the heat touch the back of her throat and work its magic all the way down into her stomach.

Glorious! It was truly the simple things that made life so wonderful, she thought, although, truth be told, everything in Beatrice's life was simple. It was all she'd ever known, and she was content.

Not everyone was so contented though. She pictured the angry priest, one newly come to that parish, complaining about the folk going to Beatrice for blessings and healing. That was the job of the Church, he said during his last sermon, exhorting the villagers to go to him when they needed succour, rather than some old 'wise woman' as he somewhat mockingly termed Beatrice.

Of course, that had started tongues wagging, with some asking in whispering tones whether Beatrice was actually a witch.

She sighed and took another drink of the creamy milk, refusing to allow the bitter memories to ruin her enjoyment of its warming effects. The previous priest, a kindly old soul named Martin, had never had any issue with Beatrice – in fact, they had been good friends. But he had died and this new fellow had turned up…

Still, his venomous words didn't seem to have had any effect on her fellow villagers so far, other than those silly rumours only the gossips bothered with, and even they didn't put much credence in them. Beatrice, a witch, ha! It was ludicrous, she was as devout a Christian as any in Nostell.

"Come up, then," she smiled, gesturing to a little black cat which was sitting on the floor, staring up at her. As she spoke, it instantly sprang into her lap, curled into a ball, and closed its eyes contentedly.

There had been the fine, though, she reminded herself, thinking again of that damned priest and his accusations. He'd actually gone to the trouble of complaining to the bishop, and he'd found Beatrice guilty of selling fake holy water. It was, obviously, a laughable suggestion – she didn't sell 'holy water', just herbal tonics and the like. She suspected the bishop had thought his priest's charges just as silly as she did, and the fine he'd imposed on her had reflected that, for it was a small one.

Unfortunately for Beatrice, even a small fine was too much for her to afford. You couldn't pay a fine with warm milk, or half a loaf of black bread. The idea of selling her cures and advice for coin had crossed her mind, but she knew doing that would only bring more ire from the churchmen.

It was a pickle, she thought, but she couldn't pay a fine with money she didn't have! She shook her head and drained the last of her milk, setting the mug down on the table as quietly as possible so as not to wake the sleeping cat in her lap.

Its slumber was rudely disturbed, though, by a sudden hard thumping on her door. Beatrice stared at it, bemused. It was snowing outside and, by her reckoning, it must be long past sunset.

The hammering came again, more urgently, louder, and the cat jumped down and scurried into a corner.

"Who's there?" she demanded, thinking it must be someone needing urgent advice on some matter of their health. A man come to ask about his pregnant wife, or someone with a bleeding wound, or—

"It's the bailiff. Open up in the name of the king!"

Beatrice sagged back into her chair. Bailiff? Now? Did they not sleep, or rest, like normal people?

"What d'you want?" she called, staring at the bolt and wondering how long it would hold if the bailiff tried to break inside.

"Payment of a fine," returned the voice outside. "I've come to collect, on behalf of the bishop."

"I thought you said you were here in the name of the king?" Beatrice demanded, eyes narrowing shrewdly. She had enjoyed catching the man out, but then a shiver of fear ran down her back.

He was lying about his purpose there. Why?

"Are you going to pay your fine, witch?"

The visitor's voice was lower now, but infinitely more menacing.

"Come back in the morning," she called back in a tremulous voice. "I'm resting just now. Haven't been well. I think I might have caught something." She thought for a moment, and then cried, "Leprosy, maybe! Like that Robert the Bruce died from!" The Scottish king had passed just a year before and rumours around England suggested he'd died from the fearsome disfiguring disease.

There was silence outside and Beatrice pictured the 'bailiff' jumping back, away from her door, terrified of catching the dreaded illness. Indeed, when he spoke again, his voice was more distant. She could hear him clearly enough, though.

"I'll ask once more: Are you going to pay your fine? Now, not tomorrow morning."

"No," she retorted angrily. "I don't have it, and you can tell the bishop, or the king, or that bloody priest, I'll never pay their fine!"

Again there was silence, and Beatrice sat, listening to the wind blowing through the cracks in the walls. The man did not speak again and, eventually, she heaved a long sigh of relief. He must have left.

Tomorrow, she would have to speak with some of the villagers – tell them of her predicament and ask them to help her with the fine in return for…Whatever she could offer. Healing, blessings, maybe even clean their houses or help with their meals…Anything.

A log cracked in the fire and she jumped, staring at the flames, trying to calm herself after the frightening visitor. There was another crack and she frowned, for, although it was unmistakeably the sound of something burning, nothing had moved in her own hearth.

Then she felt the heat overhead and looked up. God's blood, the roof was on fire!

Grasping the table, she used it to lever herself upwards, onto her feet, and then she stumbled for the door, throwing back the bolt and hurrying outside, shouting the names of her cats, calling on them to follow her. They needed no second invitation, three of them raced past her, hackles raised in terror, disappearing into the snow that was falling all around.

"Help!" she screamed towards the village. "Help! Fire!" She turned back to look at the house she'd lived in for the past fifty years, tears blurring her vision as the fire consumed the thatched roof completely, orange flames licking upwards in the night, ashes and embers floating all around as the walls too began to burn. Even if help did come from the villagers, it would be far too late.

# CHAPTER EIGHT

"Wake up! Wake up, you big hairy whoreson!"

Little John groaned and rubbed at his eyes, trying to get his bearings, wondering where the hell he was, and what all that shouting was about.

"Come out, you coward!"

He soon remembered he was at home, in his own bed, and, from the sunshine coming through the gaps in his shutters, it was daytime. There was no sign of his wife, Amber, but she was likely off running errands or seeing to some chores in town. He'd come home late the previous night after a few days away on the Sheriff's business and, clearly, had needed a lot of sleep to be waking at this late hour.

So, he knew who he was, and where he was, but what was all that noise outside?

"Come out and face us, bailiff! We know you're skulking away in there!"

From the sounds of it, there were a lot of folk in the street outside. Perhaps as many as twenty, thirty, or even more. And they wanted him, for some reason he couldn't quite understand – they weren't there to buy him drinks and feed him sweetmeats though, that much was obvious. Their cries of, "Come out!", "Wake up!", "Show yourself," and so on, continued, with one man more alarmingly shouting, "Kill him!"

He stretched his arms out over his head, rolled his neck, then stood up and, in no particular hurry, put on his trousers, boots, cloak – it was freezing out there, he could tell by the icy draught coming through the shutters along with the sunshine – and then, finally, lifted the quarterstaff that was almost as tall as he was.

Then he rinsed his mouth with some water in the jug on the table, and threw the front door open, striding out confidently and staring at those who'd come to disturb his rest.

"What do you want, you noisy bastards?" he demanded and the sight of him cowed the people gathered there. They fell silent for a moment, fearing they might be on the receiving end of the enormous quarterstaff, and then people started shouting again – mostly those hidden at the back of the crowd.

"What's going on?" Will Scaflock appeared, rather to John's relief, barging his way angrily through the crowd and striding forward to stand beside his old friend. "What have you done?"

"No idea," John said. "Woke up to this mob calling for my head."

"You burned down Beatrice's house," a man at the front of the crowd shouted. His claim was met with a chorus of agreement from behind him and hands pushed him forward to speak, although, from his frightened expression, he was wishing he'd kept his mouth shut.

"Who the hell is Beatrice?" Will demanded, looking from the man, to John, and back again.

"Our village wise-woman," the man replied, voice rising in pitch until he had to swallow and gather his composure before continuing. "Bailiff went to her house two nights ago and burned the place to the ground. She was inside it at the time, too!"

More shouts of, "Aye!" and "Kill the bastard," before John raised a hand, shaking his head in consternation.

"Where?" he asked simply.

"Nostell," the man said, pointing southeast. "You know it well, you've been there plenty times in recent years."

Yet more calls of hearty agreement.

"True," John agreed readily enough. "I do know it. But you've got the wrong man, you idiots. I was a dozen miles away from Nostell two nights ago, in Dewsbury. And the sheriff himself can vouch for it, because I was on his business at the time!"

This silenced the mob, and the expressions which had been murderous, now turned to bemusement and confusion. And then fear, as they wondered what the giant, bearded man standing before them might do. He may not have burned down Beatrice's hovel, but everyone knew he'd killed people in the past, and he was holding that enormous staff...

The crowd seemed to step backwards and even thin out in numbers somewhat. Tuck arrived then, shoving through the people much as Will had done before him – he might be a man of God, but the friar had been a wrestler in his youth and was as hardy a fighter as any man in Yorkshire.

"One of the village children came to tell me you were in trouble," the friar said when he finally stood next to John. "What's all this?"

"They thought he'd burned down some old woman's house," Will said, almost laughing at how crazy the charge sounded. Tuck didn't laugh, however. Instead, he looked at the people who were still standing before them.

"Who's the leader here?"

The man who'd stepped forward to accuse John still looked frightened, but those around him were quick to point in his direction. He'd been the one to lead the mob here after all, and it wasn't just the folk from Nostell that had come – there were also people from Horbury and Penyston there.

"Luke led us here," a woman in the front row of the group said. "He's the headman of Penyston. He sent messengers to all the villages, asking folk to join him, and come here to confront you."

"All right," John said, nodding and pointing the tip of his staff at the man she'd called Luke. "Get inside my house and we'll have a talk."

Luke seemed frozen to the spot, petrified at the suggestion he be cooped up in a house with three infamous former-outlaws.

"Oh, hurry up," Scaflock shouted, walking forward and grasping Luke by the arm. "We're not going to kill you. Unless you really annoy us." He winked at Tuck, who couldn't help smiling, and then he and John followed Will and Luke into the house.

"You want a drink?" John asked, and Luke, white-faced and nervous, nodded his thanks. Soon the four of them were seated at John's table, with weak ale, and some bread and butter laid out for John by Amber before she'd left for the morning. His belly rumbled and he broke his fast with gusto, offering some of the food to his guests although none took any. Not even Tuck.

"So," Will said to Luke. "What the hell would make you believe John could be guilty of burning down a lady's house?"

Luke swallowed some of his ale and returned Will's gaze with a bemused expression on his craggy features. "Well," he said, eyeing Tuck and John anxiously, "he *was* an outlaw, and quite an infamous one at that. I mean, he nearly killed some butcher in Darton not long ago and, if the tales about your old gang are true, John has done much worse than just setting fire to an old woman's house."

"I don't just go about the country lighting fires," John laughed. "Not even when I was a wolf's head."

"Aye," Will agreed, although he wasn't as amused as his friend. "We were *good* outlaws. We helped people!"

Luke nodded quickly. "I know, I know! But…"

"There has to be something more," Tuck said. "What, specifically, brought you to John? Did someone accuse him?"

Luke stared at his fingers, poking at a piece of dry skin on his thumb. "Yes, in a roundabout way. The thing is," he looked at John, "Beatrice's house being burned down isn't the first time a bailiff's done something similar – violent – around here lately."

John, Will, and Tuck shared a glance. This was news to them.

"Go on," Tuck urged.

"A man was visited by a bailiff in Penyston a month or so ago," Luke told them. "At night too. Collecting a fine, claimed the bailiff. But, when the man opened the door, the bailiff attacked him with his sword and killed him. Then the lawman came into the house and, right in front of the dead man's wife, stole his coin-purse before making off."

It was a disturbing story, but murder was a fairly common occurrence and it didn't shock any of the ex-outlaws.

"The lady described the bailiff," Luke said. "She got quite a good look at him, even though it was dark. She said he was a very tall fellow, with broad shoulders, unruly hair and a bushy beard."

"That does describe you," Will said, pursing his lips and examining John before turning back to Luke. "Did she describe this bailiff as being hideously ugly? If so, I think you're in trouble, John."

Little John made an obscene gesture and Tuck shook his head as if dealing with naughty children.

"What else?" the friar said, rotating his hand to make Luke continue the story.

"A lad in Horbury was attacked by someone, again claiming to be a bailiff. A woman saw them fighting outside her house and was specifically told by the large, bearded man that he was a bailiff. The dead man was, as before, robbed." He lifted his cup and drank some more. "Similar tales are going around, with this tall, bearded bailiff accosting people in the night and assaulting them or killing them before taking what he claims is due 'to the king', or 'the bishop' in the case of Beatrice."

They sat, digesting all this information, as John finished his breakfast and then, wiping crumbs from his beard, he said, "Well, it's nothing to do with me. I wouldn't rob people, and I certainly wouldn't set fire to an old woman's house."

Luke nodded sadly. "Yes, I believe you. The stories do all agree that you boys were not wicked, despite being outlaws. I even remember one winter you brought supplies to my village, because you'd stolen them from some wealthy nobleman's stores." He smiled at the memory. "Robbing the rich to help the poor. I'm sorry, John, but when people started hearing about this rogue bailiff, and the description that matched you so closely, well...You can see why it didn't take long before people started naming you as the culprit."

"Fair enough," John said. "No harm done, although you're lucky my wife wasn't about when you started shouting outside. She'd have been out there with my quarterstaff cracking heads."

Luke smiled but clearly wasn't sure whether John was joking or not. "So, er...Can you do something about it?" he asked.

"About what?"

"The bailiff that's attacking people," Luke said. "I mean, you're one of the sheriff's men, and whether this other bearded fellow is a real bailiff or not, it doesn't matter, does it? He needs to be stopped."

"I just collect fines," John said, shaking his head. "The sheriff tells me who he wants me to deal with and I do it. I don't have any official powers to investigate murders or anything like that. You'll have to ask your own bailiff or the beadle, or the coroner to deal with this. What happens outside Wakefield has nothing to do with me I'm afraid."

Luke stood up with a glum expression. "Oh well, I suppose we'd better all head home then, for I'm not sure what else to do. Thank you for your hospitality,

John, it's been nice meeting you." He bowed slightly to them all. "And you, Friar Tuck. Will." Then, guided by John, the man went out and rejoined his companions.

When the door was closed and the three friends were alone, Tuck said, "You told him you can't investigate murders. But we did exactly that last winter, with the people being killed by the Disciples of God." [1]

"That was happening near here, though," John said. "It affected us, and people from Wakefield. I mean, I was within my rights to look into that." He shook his head, remembering the strange religious sect that was led by a woman, Lady Alice de Staynton, and been responsible for the deaths of a number of acolytes in order to steal their wealth from them. John, Tuck and Will had uncovered the truth about the sect and its charismatic leader, and put an end to their crimes. "This is completely different," he muttered. "I wouldn't even know where to begin investigating it, even if I had the authority."

"Maybe so," said Tuck with a sigh. "But this man is quite clearly dangerous. I don't like the idea of him wandering about Yorkshire, killing people at will."

John nodded. "Agreed. We should get the word about town, people are not to open their doors at night to strangers, especially those claiming to be bailiffs. If anyone sees anything suspicious, raise the hue and cry."

Tuck and Will got to their feet. "I think we should all check our houses," said Scarlet. "Make sure our locks are in good order, and shutters can be fastened

---

[1] See *Sworn to God*

tight but opened easily from the inside just in case some lunatic sets alight to the place."

Tuck shook his head. "I swear, England gets worse every year. It wasn't like this when I was a lad."

Once, that would have brought a laugh from John and Will, but they were beginning to agree with Tuck. Things really were getting worse. Or maybe they were just getting older and viewing things through a nostalgic eye. Whatever the truth, they all prayed the murderous bailiff stalking the country would soon face justice.

"Oh, Farrier and his mates are going on another ghost hunt in the marshes tonight," Tuck said, turning back to John as he and Will reached the gate. "Thought I might go. What d'you think?"

John looked up at the sky, wondering if it would rain. It was cloudy but there was no hint of damp in the air, and he smiled. "All right. I think it'll be another waste of time, but it's not like I'll be doing anything else, and Amber said she'd like to see the manor house at night."

"Will?"

Scarlet shook his head and, waving, walked away in the direction of his own farmhouse. "Nah, not after hearing about that mad bailiff. I'd rather not leave Elspeth and Blase alone with someone like that on the loose."

Tuck had no children, and John's son was a young man himself now and living away, but Will had only recently remarried and been blessed with his 2-year-old son, Blase. It was completely understandable that he'd want to protect his wife and son.

Still, John thought, winking at Tuck and shouting to their departing friend, he wasn't getting off that easily. "I didn't think you'd come anyway, Scarlet. Too frightened of the ghost!"

Will's vicious retort was enough for Tuck to make the sign of the cross and head homewards himself.

As it turned out, Will had the right idea, for he spent a comfortable evening wrapped up in his cosy bed, while the ghost hunters passed an uneventful, boring hour in the marshes before trudging home, damp and disappointed. The fabled treasure would need to be found another time.

# CHAPTER NINE

Winter deepened, bringing storms as rain, wind and sleet battered the north of England. Rumours of ghosts wandering in the marshes east of Wakefield tapered off for few people were walking there at this time of year and the prospect of finding treasure seemed less immediate than that of putting food on the table the next day. Besides, the ground, wet even in summer, was completely sodden, and even those hardy souls who were most interested in catching a glimpse of the spectral Ralph de Mandeville's treasure knew it would be folly to visit the ruined manor house in the dark until the frosts dried things up.

Tales of the rogue bailiff did not abate however – in fact, it seemed more people were the victim of his attacks with every passing day.

"Do you think all these stories are true?"

Will hammered an iron nail into the board Little John was holding up against the side of the stable and stepped back to look at their handiwork. "What d'you mean?" he asked, deciding another plank was needed to complete the repair to the wall which had been damaged in the recent winds. He might not be the best farmer, but Will Scaflock took good care of his animals, and he didn't want the horses freezing because he'd neglected to make sure the stable was weatherproof. The farm had once belonged to Will's adult daughter, Beth, but her husband had secured a job in Sheffield and they'd taken their little son,

Robert, to live there while Will took over the farm here in Wakefield.

"Well," John said, lifting a second beam and holding it where Will directed. "If the stories are all true, this so-called bailiff must be able to get about the country much faster than any normal person. There was a man assaulted in Roreston a few nights ago, and the very same night another fellow was robbed and left for dead near Leeds. Both claimed a big, bearded bailiff did it."

Will hammered home a nail and then moved to the far end of the plank, lining up another, frowning as he followed John's logic. "That's too far to travel in just a few hours," he agreed. "Even on horseback."

"Exactly," John said, wincing as the shock from the hammer blows travelled through his hands and along his arms. "So, I'm guessing there's actually two of these fake bailiffs, working together."

"That'll do it," Will said, tucking his hammer into his belt and eyeing the stable wall happily. "The horses won't be too bothered by draughts now."

John stood beside him and looked at their repair. "It's squint," he said, waiting gleefully for the expected angry outburst.

"I doubt the horses will give a shit how it looks," Will retorted, refusing to allow his friend to puncture his well-earned sense of accomplishment. "Come on, my hands are numb. Let's get back to the house and warm up."

Will led the way, John following, towards his home, a spacious farmhouse with a well-kept garden and a couple of dogs which were kept outside in a rudimentary but sturdy kennel with a fence around it.

The animals watched as the two men walked past, tails wagging as Will grinned at them and ruffled their ears. They were well trained though, and didn't even attempt to jump over their fence as Will opened the door and the men went inside.

"Nice-looking animals," John noted. Will had only recently acquired the dogs and installed the kennel and this was the first time the bailiff had seen them.

"Aye," Scarlet agreed. "They're biddable enough. Best thing is, if anyone comes within fifty yards of the house they go crazy." He tapped his nose. "Amazing sense of smell. They can tell if a rat, or a fox, or a person, is nearby, and they let me know all about it."

"You worried about a visit from this – these – bailiffs?" John asked, one eyebrow raised. Will might be scared of ghosts, but living men?

Scarlet nodded though. "I lost my first wife and most of my children to a visit from a gang of murderers, remember? I won't let it happen again. The dogs'll warn me if the fake bailiffs are about and give me time to have my sword ready for them. Let's face it – I was an outlaw and they might want to see me face their 'justice'."

John laid a consoling hand on his friend's shoulder, sorry his words had brought up the painful memories for Will.

They'd just gone into the farmhouse and were about to close the door when they heard hooves pounding along the road. They looked at one another, and John gripped the hilt of his sword as Will pulled the hammer from its place in his belt and they took up positions on either side of the threshold.

The dogs were already barking madly, and Will thought about running into the back room where his wife, Elspeth, was working and looking after young Blase. All the recent talk of ghosts and murderous villains was getting to him, he thought, feeling slightly silly to be reacting in such a paranoid way to the arrival of a visitor. He and John didn't give up their posts though.

"What the hell is wrong with those dogs, Will?" Elspeth's muffled voice came through the wall behind them. "Their noise is upsetting Blase. Shut them up, for God's sake!"

"All right, my love," Scarlet shouted.

He didn't respond to the amused look John gave him, or the bailiff's mouthed, incredulous, "My love?" He was too focused on the approaching danger.

The thudding hooves came closer and closer until, at last, the horse thundered into view and, over the barking and yammering of the guard dogs, John lowered his sword and, grinning said, "It's Tuck."

Will shook his head in obvious relief and the pair walked out to meet their old friend, the dogs' barks turning to excited yelps and furiously wagging tails as they realised, from Will's demeanour, that this newcomer was no threat.

"Good," Tuck called as he cantered into the grounds and saw them waiting for him. "You're both here."

"What's happened?" John demanded, grasping the horse's bridle and holding it firm as the friar looked down at them. "Why the hurry to get here?"

"There's been another attack," said Tuck. "And this time it was in Wakefield."

"Oh, shit," John growled, shaking his head. "This is getting completely out of hand."

"Whereabouts?" Will asked.

"An old cottage on the western side of town," Tuck said, nodding in the direction he'd described. "It's pretty much derelict but it seems someone was living there."

John and Will looked at one another, puzzled. They knew the building Tuck was talking about, for it was located near the road leading to Dewsbury and could be seen easily enough by passing travellers. The house was, as the friar said, as good as derelict, with only two walls still standing. Only a desperate person would choose to seek shelter there.

"William Bywater," Tuck said, seeing the question in their eyes. "You know him?"

Will shook his head. "No," he replied. "Never heard of him. What is he, a vagrant?"

"Not just a vagrant." It was John who answered the question this time. "He's a wolf's head. Wanted for murdering a farm labourer in Leeds, along with other violent crimes and robberies. The sheriff put out an order for his arrest a couple of months ago, asking all bailiffs and foresters to be on the lookout. I assumed he'd fled to Scotland or something."

Tuck was shaking his head. "He was living right here in our own town all that time."

"God's bollocks," Will muttered. "The world's going to hell."

"So the fake bailiff managed to track down William Bywater, and attacked him?" John said.

"Aye," Tuck agreed. "Fake or not, he managed to do what no other lawmen could do."

"In this case, I don't think it matters," John snorted. "Bywater's an animal. I don't care who deals with him – he needed to be stopped before he hurt anyone else. It might not be lawful, but I won't mourn the death of a murderer."

"Are you coming inside, Tuck, or are we going to stand here looking up at you all morning?" Will turned and headed towards his door, intending to get cosy by the fire as they discussed this new development, but the friar called to him.

"No, I'm not coming in. You two need to get your horses and come along with me."

"What for?" John asked.

"Bywater isn't dead," replied the friar. "He fought back and managed to escape."

"Then he killed the bailiff?"

"No, Scarlet, but he did get a good look at his attacker. We've finally got a chance of a detailed description of the fake bailiff. Come on, mount up and let's go. He's at the alehouse being bandaged up. We can question him, and then ride out to the old cottage he was attacked in, see if we can find any clues."

Both John and Will were already on their way towards the stables.

"You said this case didn't involve you, John. Wasn't in your jurisdiction. Well, it is now!"

Elspeth appeared at the door as the three men were preparing to leave. Will quickly told her what was happening and where they were going.

"When will you be home?" she asked, but she wasn't frightened by his departure. Elspeth was a strong woman, and the dogs would warn her of any approaching danger long before it could do her or Blase any harm. Still, with all that was going on it was only sensible to be careful, especially as night fell early at this time of year.

"No idea," Will replied. "But I'll be back before dark. If the dogs start barking, you might want to let them in the house with you and lock the door until you know it's safe." He blew her a kiss. "Love you! Give Blase a hug for me. I'll see you later."

Tuck and John also waved cheerily to her and then they rode towards the centre of town, and the alehouse that was so often the hub of the entire community.

As they rode, John noticed Tuck smiling and shaking his head.

"What's funny?" he asked.

"I'm just thinking," said the friar. "These mysteries always seem to find us at the same time: winter." He pointed to the frost-rimed field they were passing and pulled his hood up over his tonsured head. "For once, I'd like to investigate one of these strange cases in the summer. When it would actually be pleasant to ride around the country, basking in the sunshine, rather than freezing our arses off in the wind and snow."

John laughed, pulling his cloak up around his neck to try and stifle the draught that was blowing down his back. "Better get used to it," he called. "Like Christmas, it seems solving a mystery has become a winter tradition for us!"

"Aye," Will agreed sarcastically. "Christmas just wouldn't be the same without some deranged criminal roaming the countryside killing folk, would it?"

# CHAPTER TEN

There was a crowd around the alehouse when they got there – news travelled fast in Wakefield and excitement like this was always a welcome diversion from the drudgery of the day. The headman, Patrick Prudhomme, was standing guard at the door and his worried expression changed to one of relief when he saw John and his companions approaching.

"There's Little John," someone shouted. "He'll sort that bastard out!"

"Don't let him escape, John," another called. "He's a murderer."

One old woman grasped John by the arm as he pushed his way through the mob. She looked about a hundred years old, with only a single tooth left and thin limbs which seemed so fragile they might break at the slightest touch.

"Bailiff," she said in a wavering, reedy voice and John had to bend to hear for she barely came up to his stomach.

"Aye, Mags?" he said kindly.

"Punch that man in the throat for me, will you?"

Will and John both laughed and pushed on as Tuck shook his head reproachfully at the elderly lady, who was now making a fist and punching the air with it, much to the crowd's delight.

"Good to see you," said Patrick as he moved aside to let the bailiff through. Little John was not the official bailiff for Wakefield, that office was held by another man, Elmer, who lived some miles away and wouldn't be able to reach the town for some days, along with the coroner. So John, a lawman with the sheriff's authority to arrest criminals, was generally the first person the villagers looked to when the hue and cry was raised in Wakefield. Will Scaflock and Tuck were obviously well known by everyone too, so they were allowed into the alehouse without question.

There were no better people to deal with murderers than those three, after all.

The injured man, William Bywater, was lying on one of the tables, a rolled-up cloak propping up his head. His own clothes were stained heavily with blood around the midriff area, and his face was deathly pale. When he saw the massive bailiff stepping into the room his face fell, for he instantly recognised John and knew any chance of escape had gone.

The barber-surgeon had left, but remaining in the alehouse with the prisoner were the innkeeper, Alexander, and a couple of sturdy young men who'd been ordered to guard the prisoner. In return, it looked like they'd been given free ale but John told them they could go. They went gladly, warmed by their drinks and the excited questions the mob bombarded them with as soon as they were outside.

"Now," said the bailiff as he sat on a stool next to Bywater and was joined at the table by Tuck and Will. "I know who you are, for our headman recognised you. You're wanted for murdering a labourer so, as soon as the sheriff's men get here in a few days, you'll be taken off to Nottingham to face his justice. There's a few other charges against you as well – you're not a very nice person, are you?"

Bywater turned his face away, staring at the far wall with an angry, defeated expression. "Well, bugger off then," he grunted. "If you don't like my company."

"Oh, we will," Tuck said. "But first you can tell us what happened."

"Why should I?" the injured man demanded. "What's in it for me? The sheriff'll hang me anyway."

"What's in it for you?" Scarlet said, standing and glaring down into Bywater's eyes. "Well, you'll get a dry room to stay in until the coroner comes to deal with this, and food enough to keep you going. On the other hand, if you don't talk to us, you'll get none of that, and a sore face as well!"

As he spoke, Will grabbed Bywater around the neck and squeezed. The man's eyes turned to John, expecting the lawman to intervene, but even Tuck didn't seem inclined to restrain Scarlet.

"All right!" Bywater gasped, choking as the pressure was released from his throat. He didn't bother complaining about his treatment for it was quite clear how things stood. As a wolf's head, an outlaw, these men could kill him if they wanted, for he no longer had the law's protection on his side. And they were obviously not in the mood to waste time questioning him. "All right, I'll talk, you bastards."

Will returned to his seat and nodded grimly. "Go on, then. What happened at the derelict cottage? Were you living there?"

"Aye," Bywater admitted, although his voice was hoarse, and they had to wait a few moments until he'd sipped some ale and was able to breathe properly again. "I've been hiding there for a while."

"How?" Tuck asked. "It's barely even got a roof!"

"I built a lean-to with branches and stuff," the prisoner replied sullenly. "There's still a couple of walls that kept the worst of the wind off and hid the light from my fire." He sat up, clutching his side as a spasm went through him, then took another drink of his ale. "Not the most comfortable way to live, but I bet you boys know all about that, eh?" He eyed them in disgust and there was no need for words for it was obvious how he felt about these three former outlaws treating him the way they were.

"Good enough for you," Scarlet said.

"What happened last night?" John asked, before Bywater became sidetracked by Will's comment.

"It was bloody freezing, again," the prisoner said. "But, as usual, I was careful not to kindle the fire until it was dark and there were no travellers on the road to spot the light. I cooked a sparrow I'd managed to snare—"

"A sparrow?" Will demanded incredulously. "A sparrow?" And he laughed mockingly at Bywater's hunting skills until Tuck told him to shut up so they could get on with the story.

"I ate my supper," Bywater continued, "and sat before the fire, warming myself. Or trying to, at any rate." He shivered, remembering the bitter cold and how it had felt on his skin; how it gnawed at one's entire body and spirit. His eyes glazed over, as if he was lost in the memory, and then he looked up with a start, taking in the warmth and light of the alehouse, breathing deeply as if drawing it all into himself.

John watched him, surprised but not shocked by the man's strange behaviour. As an outlaw himself, and, latterly, a bailiff, he'd come across all sorts of odd characters. "Go on," he said, and Bywater nodded, licking his lips.

"I was staring into the flames, trying to make my body believe it was warmer than it really was, when there was a crack. At first, I thought it was just one of the logs splitting in the fire, but I became sure it had come from outside the house." He stopped talking and sat on the table, dangling his legs from it like a child and rubbing his side.

"And?" Tuck prompted.

Bywater blinked and seemed to remember where he was again. "I lifted my knife, and pulled out one of the burning branches from the fire, then I stood up and waited behind the wall." He smiled, a strangely disturbing curling of his lips, clenching his fist as if it held the weapons still. "The big bastard came right into the house, sword drawn." He chuckled. "Thought I was behind the fire. Thought he'd caught me unawares." His mirth evaporated and he said, "I shoved the burning branch into his face and stabbed him with my knife. I got him with the fire, right in the beard, ha! I can still smell it burning and see the look on his face."

Tuck, John, and Will all looked at one another hopefully. Bywater had got a good look at his attacker's face then. The other witnesses had only managed hasty glimpses in the dark, nothing detailed, yet this man had shoved a burning brand into the attacker's face!

"Somehow, he blocked my knife," Bywater went on. "Knocked it aside with his sword, and then, before I could recover and try to get him again, he stabbed me in the side. I fell back against the wall," he said, holding his wound and gritting his teeth. "But his face must have been hurting bad, 'cause he didn't come at me again."

"Did he say anything?" John asked.

"Oh aye," Bywater said, head tilting as he nodded. "He said he was 'the bailiff' and he'd come to deliver justice to me for my crimes. Some other nonsense about 'in the name of the king' too." He sniggered, a cold and mirthless sound. "I could see he was hurting, and I was up for a fight, thought it would warm me up if nothing else. So I went for him again, shoving the branch at him and lunging with the knife. Ha! He actually screamed although I don't think I managed to hit him. Then he ran off." He looked down at his side, touching the dried blood and the tear in his cloak. "It was only once he was long gone that I realised how badly injured I was. Knew I'd die if I didn't get some help so…" He shrugged and raised his head to peer at Alexander behind the bar. "Managed to drag myself here, hoping the fat innkeeper there might patch me up."

"Got you help, didn't I?" Alexander shouted. "Got you bandaged up. Probably saved your worthless life. Shouldn't have bloody bothered, should I?"

"What did this 'bailiff' look like?" John demanded, drawing attention back to the matter at hand.

Bywater thought about it, then said, "Tall. Taller than me, and I'm not exactly small. Beard. Bushy hair." He smirked. "Looked a lot like you, actually. Maybe it *was* you."

"Shut up, you fool," Tuck spat. "You said you shoved a burning branch in the man's face. John has no marks on him, so it clearly was not him."

"Aye," Bywater said, still smiling irritatingly. "I suppose so. He wasn't as big either. I think he might have been pretending to be you, though. Maybe it's someone you've wronged in the past. I'll bet that's a long list of folk, eh? You should watch your back, bailiff. You all should."

John frowned. He had not considered any of this until now. Maybe Bywater was right. He'd certainly crossed a lot of people in his life, on both sides of the law. Dangerous people. Could all this be a plot to frame him? Was it just a coincidence that the fake bailiff apparently looked like him?

But if some enemy wanted to harm John, why not just attack him directly? Or, if not him, Amber, or his son?

He couldn't make sense of it. They still didn't have enough information to go on, but at least they knew one thing now: The man they were hunting, or one of them at least, didn't just look like John, he now had fresh burn marks on his face, and a badly singed beard. It wasn't a lot, but it was a start. There couldn't be too many people wandering around Yorkshire who fitted that description.

"I think we've heard enough," John said, looking from Tuck to Will in case they had anything more to ask. "I'd hoped you would give us a clear, detailed description of the man we're after, but you've not been much help."

"Help?" Bywater demanded. "Why should I help you any more than I have, lawman? Will you let me go? No, of course not."

John didn't bother replying, just looked at his friends to see if they had anything more to ask before they left the man to his fate.

Will nodded. He had one more question for William Bywater. "Did you murder the labourer?"

The prisoner answered without hesitation. "Aye. No point in denying it – I killed the farmhand, and was just about to do for his son as well, when another couple of labourers turned up. They recognised me and chased me off." He sighed as if all the weight of the world was upon him. "If those two hadn't turned up when they did, I'd have got away with it."

"Why?" Tuck asked.

"Money, of course," Bywater replied. "I needed a drink and some food, and I wanted their coin purses so I could afford it."

"You never thought of doing an honest day's work yourself?" Scarlet asked in disgust.

"No," Bywater answered with a bored shrug. "Not really. Tried it a couple of times, but both my parents died when I was young so I didn't have much chance to learn a trade or anything like that. Not much money out there for a man like me." He returned Will's stare coolly, unblinking. "It's a hard life for a poor boy, as you damn well know. So, I did what I could with the tools God gave me." He lifted his hands and made squeezing motions with them while smiling viciously.

"Enjoy your last few days of life," John muttered, leading his friends towards the door and the waiting

Patrick Prudhomme. "The sheriff will deal with you soon enough."

Tuck paused as they reached the door, looking back at Bywater sorrowfully. "I'll pray for your soul," he told the prisoner, and they left him to the headman.

# CHAPTER ELEVEN

St Mary's was packed with villagers, there to celebrate Mass on St Martin's Day, November 11th. It was cold, even inside the church, and the congregation frequently blew on their hands or rubbed them together to try and get some heat into them. Some men even stamped their feet to warm up, receiving angry looks from their neighbours.

Father Myrc was used to it of course, for many of his flock were old and felt the cold terribly. He was just glad so many of them made the effort to come and hear his sermons, bring offerings of bread and wine, and drop a coin or two into the collection plate. Especially at this time of year, when so many poor people struggled to feed themselves, the priest would share out some of the alms with those who needed help the most.

The Wakefield folk were quite generous, the priest always said, compared to some. Indeed, this very building had been recently renovated and extended, all paid for by Robin Hood himself, who'd grown up in the village. The young man had decided to use the money he'd made as an outlaw to give back to the community that he and his family had belonged to for generations.

This particular day, Martinmas, was a feast day. Later there would be games and revelry, and the local children would dress in rags before going around the houses, singing and asking for alms. Rents would be paid too, as was traditional, and many animals would be slaughtered to provide food for the people over the hard winter months.

This was all running through Little John's mind as he rubbed his numb hands and listened to the Latin words Father Myrc was speaking. The church was a fine building, he thought – not too big, but sturdily built, and well-appointed with paintings on the walls depicting scenes from the bible. The candles placed in alcoves didn't just look pretty either, their yellow flames gave at least an illusion of warmth for the congregation gathered to stand beneath the vaulted ceiling.

He breathed in, appreciating the smell of incense, as the priest began the hymn, *Gloria in Excelsis Deo* and everyone joined in, more or less enthusiastically. Amber nudged him and he raised his voice reluctantly for this kind of singing wasn't really for him, which his wife knew very well. John much preferred the bawdy songs more suited to the alehouse or the forest of Barnsdale.

Suddenly the door to the church burst open, bringing with it a gust of fresh, cold air, and a pale-faced woman of about sixty. From her expression it was clear something terrible had happened, and John, who knew the lady fairly well, immediately went to her.

"What's happened, Mabel?" he asked, taking her arm and helping her to the side of the room where there was a bench for older and infirm members of the congregation to rest on during Mass. She collapsed onto the smooth, dark wood and started to sob immediately.

"It's Hugh," she said, speaking quietly through her tears, although everyone in the church was silent, listening to what she was saying. Father Myrc was walking towards them now, his stoic presence seeming to give Mable strength as she looked up and saw him coming.

"What about him?" John asked, knowing Hugh was the lady's husband. "Where is he?"

"He's...dead!" she cried, and dissolved into another fit of sobbing as the villagers all gasped and murmured in surprise. Hugh and Mabel were neither liked or disliked, particularly. They were a quiet couple who mostly kept to themselves, making few friends and even less enemies. They were part of the fabric of the community, however, and the man's sudden death was rather a shock.

Amber came to join them and put her arms around the tearful woman for she was shaking from a combination of the cold and shock. John moved along the bench to let Father Myrc sit down and take Mabel by the hand as she tried to recount what had happened that morning.

"We went to the ruined house in the marsh," she said, haltingly, snuffling and wiping her nose as she spoke. "Just to have a look when it was light outside."

John was frowning. The idea of the pair, both in their sixties as Hugh was even older than Mabel, searching for treasure – for that was certainly the real reason for their visit – seemed strange to the bailiff. Surely they had work they should be doing, instead of wasting time visiting the marshes to look for some apocryphal, ancient hoard of coins.

"Did something happen there?" Father Myrc asked softly. "To Hugh?"

"Did he fall into the moat?" someone in the congregation called, not unkindly. "It's horrible that water, all green and—"

"Shut up, you bloody oaf," another member of the flock shouted. "Let the woman speak!"

"Shut up yourself!"

John rose to his full, imposing height and glared at the man, who instantly fell silent.

"No," Mabel said, almost whispering now as her sobs lessened and a cold, almost detached calm came over her. "He didn't fall in the moat. We saw the ghost."

Again there were gasps, and loud, excited chattering amongst the people who'd quite forgotten the Mass by now. Mabel waited for them to grow quiet before continuing.

"Outside one of the old storehouses," she said. "We weren't sure about going into the main house, because it's so badly ruined, so we were looking in the outbuildings. They're only on one level, most of them, so it's not as dangerous." She looked up, staring ahead as if seeing the scene in her mind's eye. Living it over again. "We saw a dark, hooded figure approaching through the marshes. Oh, God above, I'll never forget it. Hideous, half-hidden by the heavy mist." She shuddered and started to sob again. "It just glided right through the marsh, across the moat and disappeared into the house. It was so frightening."

"But," Father Myrc asked, squeezing Mabel's hand gently. "What happened to Hugh?"

"Well," she said, looking at him from red-rimmed eyes. "He was terrified. Collapsed on the ground holding his chest and...He wouldn't wake up. I stayed with him for a while, too scared to move, and then I ran here."

"The ghost killed him!" someone shouted, and others added their own near-hysterical voices to the growing hubbub.

"Pray for us all, Father Myrc! God save us!"

John looked at Amber, who nodded to tell him she would remain with Mabel until she calmed down. And then the bailiff walked out of the church and wandered along the road to the alehouse. Patrick, the headman, would see to recovering Hugh's body and having it brought back to the village for burial.

John knew very well how these things always went, and he had no interest in listening to the villagers working themselves into a frenzy of gossip and rumour and exaggeration. By this time tomorrow half the settlements in Yorkshire would know all about the crazed ghost in Wakefield, murdering an innocent old man where he stood.

He went inside the alehouse and asked Alexander for a drink.

"What d'you think really happened?"

The bailiff turned, freshly poured mug of ale halfway to his lips. Will Scaflock joined him at the table as the innkeeper moved to pour another drink.

"Who knows," John shrugged, taking a long pull and wiping the foam from his beard. "They probably saw an animal and their imaginations ran riot, what with all the stories going about just now. Hugh wasn't a young man, and Mabel said herself there was a heavy mist."

"Aye," Will replied, gratefully accepting his own mug from Alexander who went back to rubbing tables with his grubby cloth.

"Poor Mabel will have a hard Christmas this year," John said, and the pair sat in thoughtful silence, wondering what the hell was going on in their usually sleepy village.

# CHAPTER TWELVE

Margaret Carpenter, better known to the people of Pontefract as Meggy, was tired. She felt like she'd been awake, and working, for days, which wasn't far from the truth. She wanted to cry but couldn't even summon the energy to do that as she looked down at her infant son, asleep in his small bed.

At twenty-five Meggy was still pretty and looked her age, but she felt much older. Used up, almost, as if all the energy, all the life, had been sucked from her. As she watched her son sleeping, however, she managed a smile. Little Thomas really was the thing that kept her going every day.

Six months ago, her husband, Fulk, had been taken by a fever. He was only the same age as Meggy, so it had been a terrible shock when he'd died. Not only because they'd been childhood sweethearts, but because his death had left Meggy and her son with no source of income. The sale of Fulk's shop, and the few items of stock within, had put food on their table for a while but, eventually, there was no money left and Meggy had been forced into the world's oldest profession: prostitution.

It was degrading, and painful both physically and mentally, and she despised it, but it paid, and allowed her to feed and clothe Thomas. She'd fallen into it one day when she'd been forced to beg in the streets and a man had made her an offer which, although terrified and sickened, she'd felt she had to accept. Word had soon got around town and more men came to her. Soon enough it was a regular thing, but the men she was dealing with were not wealthy, so they couldn't afford to pay her much. Just enough to get by, and never enough to let her get out of this terrible life.

Her neighbours knew of her predicament – knew she was desperate. None had ever offered to help her mainly because, again, they didn't have much themselves. But the hard stares of the women in particular, looking down on her for selling herself for a few coins, made Meggy sick. How dare they judge her, when not one had done anything to help her support herself? What was she supposed to do? Let Thomas starve?

Now she did sit on the edge of the bed and cry. She missed Fulk so much, and the life they'd had before his cruel passing. What kind of future could she offer her son now? Or herself? God, she was not even in her thirties!

Fear hit her then. Would men still pay for her when she was older, lined and haggard, not as firm as she was now? She drew in a deep, shuddering sigh and forced herself to calm down. That was a fear for the future. For now, she had a few coins from her last customer and some bread and cheese for their breakfast in the morning.

She looked at Thomas again and smiled, part of her wishing she could wake him just to feel his little arms tight around her neck in a loving embrace. That would be selfish of her though, so she contented herself with simply watching him for a moment longer, and then she took off her boots and prepared for bed herself.

There was a knock on the door and she almost burst out crying again. *Not another customer*, she thought, feeling sick in her stomach at the thought of allowing another man to use her that night. Especially with Thomas so close-by. *Some drunk stumbling home from the alehouse at closing time*, she thought, knowing she couldn't afford to turn work away.

As her hand closed upon the latch, though, she hesitated. Drunks were sometimes belligerent towards her. Violent. They thought their money allowed them not only to have sex with her, but to hit her too. She would not have Thomas waking up and seeing some drunk knocking his mother about in their home.

The knock came again, and she quickly took out the sharp knife she used for cutting her food, slipping it into her woollen sock as she unlocked the door and opened it to the visitor.

"Yes?" she asked, peering into the dark street, not recognising the slim, hooded figure in front of her.

"Margaret Carpenter?"

She nodded at the gruff question. "Aye. What do you want?"

"You're the prostitute?"

Flushing in anger, she nodded again. "Hurry up, I don't have all night. And keep your noise down, my little boy is asleep there."

"I'm a bailiff," the visitor said in a low voice. "You know you're breaking the law?"

"No I'm not," she replied, confused by this unexpected turn in the conversation.

"Well, maybe not," the man said. "But there *should* be a law against what you're doing. It's immoral."

Amazed, Meggy said, "Did you come here to empty your balls, or to save my soul, bailiff?" Then she hesitated. There were stories going around about fake bailiffs, visiting people in the night and—

"Whatever money you have," the man said, still speaking quietly, as if he didn't want to wake the child. "Give it to me. Think of it as a fine. And, in future, find a respectable way to earn your coins."

The months of pain and sorrow and humiliation and fear seemed to crowd in upon her at that moment. He was robbing her! The money she'd worked so hard to get, with the weight of that fat, old fishmonger crushing the wind out of her earlier...This bailiff was going to steal it from her.

He was standing very close to her now, and rage filled her. She leaned down, drew out the knife in her sock, and plunged it into the man's ribs.

The visitor saw the blow coming, but not in time to completely evade it, and Meggy felt warm liquid on her hand. When she tried to stab the man again the blade caught in his cloak and, slick with blood, it slipped out of her fingers.

"You bitch," the bailiff snarled. "All you had to do was pay the fine and I'd have left you alone!"

Meggy was frightened now, but her heart was racing and she knew she had to protect herself and Thomas, so she threw herself at the man, screaming and pounding her fists against him. He was strong though, and tall, and he easily swatted her aside. As she fell, her head struck the doorframe and, with a horrible crack, she collapsed, unmoving.

The bailiff stared at her, knowing instantly that she was dead. Neck broken. He pulled his gaze away from her and looked up, into the eyes of the boy in the little bed.

"Oh, Christ," the man moaned, clutching his injured side, and then he turned and ran, stumbling, out of the door and into the night. The high, terrible cry of loss and terror followed him into the woods at the edge of town and even when he was far from Pontefract the man could still hear that tortured wail.

# CHAPTER THIRTEEN

William Bywater was taken away to Nottingham a few days later, once the coroner and Wakefield's bailiff arrived and completed their investigation. They didn't find out anything more than Little John had, and he, of course, shared what he knew with them. In turn they told him the sheriff gave his blessing for John to do what he could to apprehend the fake bailiff, or bailiffs, who were causing so much mayhem in his shires.

Targeting wanted criminals was one thing, no-one had an issue with that, not even the law, but burning down houses simply because the inhabitant was accused of being a witch, or murdering someone over unproven allegations of theft, couldn't be tolerated.

The recent heavy rains and storms had finally passed as December approached, giving way to frosts and winds that stripped the trees completely bare of their summer foliage. That meant a return to the earlier visits to the ruined manor house in the marsh, as Farrier and his friends hoped their cold vigils would bring a glimpse of some spectre that might lead them to the fabled treasure. So far, only some vague lights had been spotted, some shadowy figures, odd noises…Nothing to entice John, Tuck or Will to join the ghost hunters though.

They were more interested in hunting down the rogue bailiffs, although, despite circulating the description Bywater had given, and the fact their quarry must have a noticeably burned face, the attacks continued unabated. In fact, it seemed the perpetrators had been shocked by the encounter with William Bywater and decided to focus on 'easier' targets – ones that might not fight back with such vigour, hence the recent attack on the prostitute in Pontefract.

That hadn't gone well for the bastard either, John mused, pondering the garbled story he'd heard from a traveller regarding that case. Stabbed by the woman, and badly, judging by the trail of blood he'd left behind. Good. With any luck the wound would kill the bastard.

In truth, John had been a little surprised that Sir Henry, the sheriff, hadn't taken more of an interest in the attacks but he had a lot to deal with at that time, as did all the powerful men in England. Young King Edward had finally given his regent, Roger Mortimer, a trial, where he'd been accused of many crimes, including murdering Edward's own father. His guilt was never in doubt and the disgraced nobleman had been taken from the Tower of London and dragged behind a pair of horses to Tyburn, where he was stripped and hanged like a common criminal.

With all of this going on, it was probably understandable that the sheriff had left the crimes of a fake bailiff to be dealt with by his subordinates.

"John! Amber!"

They turned to see Farrier waving from the door of his workshop, smiling, so they altered their course – they'd been heading to the bakers to get some flour – and strode over to talk with the young man.

"Busy?" the bailiff asked, noting the hammer in Farrier's hand.

"Aye. Got a lame horse with me just now – bloody owner always does this. Leaves it too long before he comes to have me change the shoes and by that time the poor beast's limping." He shook his head. "Never mind that, though. Listen, we're going to the ruined house again tonight. You know the old stories all said the ghost appeared more around Christmastime. Well, that's not far off now and some of the villagers have reported hearing screams and moans and seeing lights in the ruins again."

John nodded, feigning interest. His earlier visits to the place had been so boring that he did not believe anyone would ever see a genuine wraith stalking the marshes. He was more worried about the very real, very dangerous men claiming to be bailiffs.

"You want to come along? Your presence would make some of the more nervous in our group feel somewhat safer."

Frowning, John couldn't help but laugh. "My presence? I can't fight a ghost. You'd be better asking Tuck, or Father Myrc. Battling evil spirits is their business, not mine."

"Oh, the priest is already coming," Farrier said. "And I'll ask Tuck if I see him. But I'm not talking about you fighting the ghost – it's these attacks that have been going on that's making people anxious." He grinned. "With you there, I reckon we'd have no reason to be fearful of any earthly danger, and it'd let us concentrate on looking for, you know, strange phenomena."

Not wanting to offend the man, but not really interested in another dark, cold vigil when he could be enjoying a warmed ale before his own fire with his wife, he hesitated. "Are you going inside the place? I might be tempted to come along if you do. Sitting about in the damp, waiting for something to happen, that's not really my thing. But if you were going inside, well, that might be exciting."

Farrier blanched. He obviously took the ghost stories very seriously, believing them to be completely true.

"What's wrong?" John demanded with a laugh. "You're a big lad. You've got a big hammer and, if Father Myrc is coming, and maybe the friar too, well, what are you so frightened of? Surely some of your group have the balls to go into the house. You're wanting to find the ghost's hidden stash of gold, aren't you? Well, how d'you expect to do that if you won't even go inside the building?"

"Don't be mean," Amber muttered, nudging John with her elbow.

"I'm no coward," Farrier protested, then, seeing John's eyebrow raised sceptically, said more forcefully, "I'm not! But you can't battle a ghost with this." He shook the heavy hammer in his hand. "But...All right then. We'll go into the ruins, if you and Tuck will come with us. You're more than welcome too, Amber."

John grinned. "Fine, we'll come, won't we?"

Amber nodded. "Why not? It'll be fun."

"Make sure you take some torches, or lamps," John told Farrier. "I want to go into the house, but not without some light to see where we're going."

Farrier and the bailiff nodded, smiling at one another.

"See you at sundown then," said Farrier. "And don't forget to bring Will Scarlet if he'll come, and especially Tuck. He could even bring his bible along, or some holy water."

John waved and walked off towards the baker's, at the end of the long main street in the village. "Bible. Holy water," he muttered to Amber with a wry smile. "Tuck's more likely to bring some bread and a full aleskin. And they'll probably be more useful!"

"Don't be so sure," his wife said, reprovingly. "I've never heard of a ghost being scared away by a loaf of bread."

"You've never seen Tuck wielding a loaf then!"

# CHAPTER FOURTEEN

In the afternoon, John rode the short distance to Will Scaflock's farm, to ask if he wanted to join them on the ghost/treasure hunt. Or, if not Will, Elspeth might come along instead, since she was friends with Amber and both John and Tuck would hopefully be there to accompany them. Couldn't have the village gossips talking about the women going about alone after all!

When he got there, however, John found his friend with hammer in hand again, battering nails into door and window frames. Young Blase was running about nearby, both of the new dogs racing after him, barking playfully. Elspeth was hanging out washing which was already steaming in the sunshine despite the cold, and she waved cheerily when she saw John.

"What are you doing now?" the bailiff asked Will, returning Elspeth's wave before dismounting and tethering his great horse to the post in the yard. "I didn't think the storm had done *that* much damage."

Will wiped sweat from his brow, breathing out heavily for, although the ground was frosty, the sun was making it warm for a man doing physical labour. "It's the dogs," he said. "I'm starting to think we should never have got them."

John frowned. This sounded ominous. "What d'you mean?"

"They've been barking during the night, and, when I've tried to go out to check what's there, Elspeth holds me back. It's making her and the boy nervous and, frankly, me too."

"They'll just be smelling rats or foxes or the like," John said, trying to sound reassuring.

Will nodded and turned back to the window he was standing beside, hammering a nail into the hinge of the shutter on the left side before adding another, then moving onto the second shutter. "Aye, probably. If we didn't have the dogs we'd be none the wiser, but the fact they've been barking when these fake bailiffs are about…Well, I thought I'd just make sure the house is as secure as possible." He sighed, breath misting in the air. "I don't think it's rats or foxes we're hearing – it sounds like something bigger. Like, man-sized."

"Come on, now, Will," said John firmly. "Even if those fake bailiffs decided to attack you for some reason, they'd have to be crazy to come here in the night. For one thing, they'd have to deal with the dogs, and for another, everyone in Yorkshire knows who you are. There's not many who'd be willing to get into a fight with you."

It was quite true; John wasn't just trying to make his friend feel better. Will's skill in battle was legendary and, of the three remaining members of Robin Hood's gang living in Wakefield, Scarlet was the one least likely to take prisoners. John or Tuck might look to incapacitate an attacker if possible, but Will wouldn't hesitate to kill someone who was there to harm him or his family.

"You know as well as I do, John," Scarlet replied, stooping to pick up a nail he'd dropped onto the frozen grass. "There's *always* someone stupid, or angry, or drunk enough to start a fight they're unlikely to win. A lot of the houses around here would be easy to break into as well. These bailiffs, or whatever they are, might think mine will be the same. They'll get a surprise if they do."

"Aye, that's a fair point," John said, stroking his beard thoughtfully. "Remember that young lad from Elton, I think it was? Tore up a whole house and carried it off in sections because he thought the people living in it owed him money or something! Took 'house breaking' to the extreme, that one."

"Wattle and daub," Will said, grinning. "Not the sturdiest of building materials – he had to take it back and rebuild it, didn't he? But my house isn't as insubstantial as that."

He hammered the retrieved nail into the next shutter, shaking the wood to check it was solid before tucking the tool into his belt and giving John his full attention. "What did you come for anyway? Just a visit?"

Amber had finished hanging the laundry and came to join them now, hooking her arm affectionately in Will's and looking at the bailiff.

"Well," John replied, smiling at them. "I was going to ask if you, or Elspeth, wanted to come with some of us to the old ruined manor in the marshes again. One of you could come – Amber will be with us too this time – while the other would stay here to look after Blase. We're going inside the building this time, it should be…interesting, if nothing else. But I'm guessing you'll not be tempted now."

Elspeth looked concerned, but Will shook his head firmly. "Nah. I'm glad you've all finally found your balls and are going into the place instead of hiding outside like frightened children, but I'm not leaving the farm alone at night until these madmen are caught."

John looked closely at Will's face and saw just how anxious his old friend was. These noises in the night had really spooked him.

"We're not imagining it," Elspeth said levelly. "The dogs smell, or hear something first, but then, in between the barks, we can hear something outside too. Will wanted to go out last night and deal with it, but I was frightened he'd get hurt and then whoever was out there would come for Blase."

It was quite clear their fears were real and, in that moment, John made a decision.

"Listen," he said. "I'll stay here with you tonight. We can take turns on watch and, if the dogs start their noise, we can go out together, Will, and find what-, or whoever is bothering them."

"What about your treasure hunting?" Will asked.

"They'll just have to go without me. I think the real threat of danger to your family is more important than protecting Farrier and his companions from some long-dead nobleman. Besides, they'll be perfectly safe – they'll have Tuck to look after them. He's almost as tough as me."

He winked at Elspeth, but she cocked her head on one side thoughtfully and said, "But Will's always telling me about the times you wrestled Tuck when you were outlaws. He says the friar managed to put you on your arse more times than you beat him."

Scarlet laughed and John shook his head as he walked over to his patiently waiting horse.

"Maybe you should ask Tuck to come and protect you tonight then," he called petulantly as he rode back towards town, but he smiled and waved farewell to them as they waved back. "See you in a while. Have some fresh ale warmed or I really will be offended!"

# CHAPTER FIFTEEN

"Hold the lamp up higher, by God. I can hardly see my feet in front of me!"

The voice was a hiss in the night, swallowed up almost instantly by the freezing, oppressive atmosphere of the marshes. Farrier was leading the small party of ghost hunters towards the ruined house, and their nerves were frayed already, despite the fact they were still not even inside the building.

Friar Tuck had agreed to come, and he patted his trusty cudgel to reassure himself – it was safely tucked into the cord around his cassock and he knew very well how to use it. The weapon was decades old and had been used to incapacitate many people in that time, including Robin Hood's predecessor, Adam Gurdon. The old outlaw leader had thought he could take on the friar when the two parties first met, and Tuck had soon shown he was no pushover.

Still, a cudgel wouldn't be much use against ghosts, so Tuck and Wakefield's priest, Father Myrc, were proudly displaying wooden crosses around their necks and the latter was muttering quiet prayers of supplication, asking God and the saints for protection on their eldritch quest this night.

Someone stubbed their toe on a branch sunk into the soft grass and let out a terrified squeal. This in turn made Little John's wife, Amber, laugh.

"Oh, for goodness' sake," she said. "Stop acting like babies."

The man who'd squealed grinned sheepishly at her and gripped his hatchet tighter. Although none of them really thought their weapons would work against spectres, it gave them confidence to carry them. Like a man walking into battle against a hundred enemy longbowmen, it made people feel better to have even a leather gambeson as protection, as ineffectual as it would surely be.

There were eight of them, including Tuck, Father Myrc, Amber and Farrier. All carried either a weapon or an oil lamp. They'd headed for the marshes as soon as the sun began to set, with Little John heading off to join Will for their own night-time vigil.

Tuck had been the oldest of the ghost-hunting party although, at fifty, he was as fit and vital as any of the others. He was content to let Farrier lead the way, for this was the younger man's adventure, but Farrier believed so deeply in the ghost of Ralph de Mandeville that he couldn't hide his fears as they stepped cautiously across the damp ground towards the derelict house.

The winter frosts had dried up the worst of the pungent, green water, and what was left sparkled almost merrily in the moonlight and the glow from the lamps. Still, no-one wanted to make a misstep and put their foot into a deeper part of the marsh so they walked carefully, taking their time and making sure to step only on the firmer ground Farrier was leading them across.

To the left and right was mostly just more marsh, with long reeds and grass showing vaguely in the gloom. Trees were visible a little way off, but the dominant part of the scene was the house itself.

Lights had been reported from some of the windows again recently, but right now nothing showed – all was black within.

"Look," said Amber, lifting her lamp and pointing at the front entrance which lay up a short flight of steps. "The doors have rotted away. It's like a big mouth, inviting us in to be swallowed up."

"Oh, don't say that," a young girl named Lily muttered fearfully. "I don't want to think of things like that. It makes the house seem like its alive."

"Yes, I think things like that are better left unsaid," Father Myrc agreed, staring at his feet as they negotiated more fallen branches that were trapped in the sucking marsh. "We must concentrate on crossing the moat."

"It's hardly a moat," Tuck said. "Not really."

"It's water that surrounds the house, isn't it?" Farrier said. Unlike the friar, he hadn't seen castles and manor houses with proper, deep and wide moats that acted as a real defensive barrier to invading forces. To Farrier, the ruined house's moat – six feet wide and probably one or two feet deep – was hugely impressive. Only the wealthiest of men could pay to have such a thing incorporated into the building plans for his home. And to divert the river to fill it…Well, Ralph de Mandeville might have been a villain, but he was obviously incredibly rich.

It all added to the romance for Farrier and his fellows. It was probably just as well they couldn't see the green sludge that passed for water though – or the things that might be living in it…

From somewhere far away there came the sound of dogs barking and everyone froze. Not because they feared the dogs, but because they wanted the silence to return. Silence could be frightening, but it also meant an enemy couldn't sneak up on you without being heard. The excited barking, although distant, might mask an approaching footstep.

So, they waited, all in a line leading towards the drawbridge, which was down and, incredibly, appeared intact. The metal frame had presumably protected the wood from the damp, although Tuck eyed it with trepidation, praying the thing would take their weight on both the journey in *and* back out. He didn't fancy being stuck in that shell of a house until someone could come along and help them out if the drawbridge collapsed. Wading through the freezing waters on a night like this would not make for a pleasant return journey to Wakefield.

The barking stopped at last and, with glances at one another, they started moving again, treading warily, senses straining.

"Be careful here," said Farrier, reaching the drawbridge and using the long axe-handle in his right hand to prod the wood. It did not crumble wetly as Tuck half expected, just resounded with a dull thud and then Farrier, steeling himself, moved carefully across it. His eyes moved up and down and it was obvious he was far more frightened of something coming out of the open front doorway than falling through into the moat, but he walked quickly across and beckoned the others to follow.

"Jesus, what's that?" Lily screeched and recoiled from the oil lamp Father Myrc was holding up, her eyes wide with fright as everyone else raised weapons and lamps and felt the blood suddenly pounding in their veins.

"What?" Amber hissed irritably, seeing nothing in the direction Lily was staring. "What's wrong?"

"It's…" The girl reached out and a smile of pure relief lit her face as something soft and white flitted gently down onto her hand, catching the meagre light as it did so. "Snowing," she finished. "I'm sorry," she mumbled in response to the angry glares turned upon her. "I just saw something in the corner of my eye and it gave me a fright."

Tuck rolled his eyes, although he was as relieved as any of them that there was no danger. Of the other three men in the party only Edward looked like he'd be useful if they were faced with a confrontation, and even he was only average in height and build. Simon was small, with a bowl cut hairstyle and poor eyesight, while Eric was about sixty, tall, bald, and more of a scholar than a brawler.

Still, the friar mused as Farrier led them all into the crumbling building, they weren't there for a fight. They were there to, hopefully, find evidence of Ralph de Mandeville's ghostly presence.

To their right was a flight of stairs, surprisingly intact. Mostly, at least. They all looked up into the inky darkness it led to, wondering what might be on the floor above. This particular part of the house still had some of its roof left, so no moon or stars were visible, just silent darkness and a sense of foreboding which everyone, even Tuck, felt.

"Should we go up?" Father Myrc asked, fingers touching his cross.

"Yes," said Amber. "We're here now. We should check everywhere for…" She trailed off and ended with a shrug. Of them all, Tuck noted, Amber seemed the least frightened, although even she was not fully at ease. How could anyone be in a place like this?

"Let's leave it until last," Farrier suggested. "The stairs look a bit rickety. We'll explore this level first, eh? Then head down to the basement, if it's not flooded." He spoke in hushed tones, as had the others, fearful, perhaps, of disturbing the ghost's peace. Or just respectful of the old building and the people who'd lived out their lives there over generations.

There was a doorway to the left, and Tuck went through, grasping his cudgel but not drawing it from his belt. He did lift the oil lamp in his left hand higher though, its pale glow casting long, moving shadows across the walls and debris which lay scattered about the floor. The floor above had collapsed at the far end of this room, and even the roof was gone. The twinkling stars somehow seemed reassuring.

Lily walked past him, using her lamp to examine everything. It looked to be mostly old furniture, rotten and falling apart. The hearth had not played host to any warming fire for decades although the remains of that last blaze could still be seen, as could the iron implements that had once been used to keep it fed and burning.

Tuck remained at the door as the others took their turn to look about the room, the visible sky and unshuttered, gaping windows making this room at least seem much less intimidating than the dark stairway.

Soon enough, however, they were filing back into the hallway for there was nothing of interest in the room.

"Onwards, then?" Farrier asked, forcing a smile and staring along the narrow hallway which had at least two doors at the far end.

"Lead the way," Eric said, and using a sleeve he wiped his bald head which Tuck could see was damp with sweat, despite the fact it was absolutely freezing in the house.

They went forward, but something made Tuck stop in his tracks. What was it? He wasn't sure, but something seemed off. Had he heard a noise? Felt a breeze from an unexpected direction? What?

And then he realised, he was smelling woodsmoke. Not the fresh, welcoming scent of a merrily burning fire, but the stale, lingering, almost damp smell of a fire that had been recently extinguished. It was a completely normal, common thing to smell which is why no-one seemed to have noticed it, but, as Tuck thought now, it was out of place in this derelict house. It had not burned in the hearth they'd just looked at, so, some other nearby room.

Did ghosts light fires? It was not a pleasant thought.

Farrier had his hand on the door at the far end of the hall, when there came the wholly unexpected sound of someone, or something, groaning.

"Oh, holy Christ!" muttered Simon, squinting into the darkness and stepping back a few paces, away from the door for the groan had seemed to come from the other side of the rotting old barrier.

"What was that?" Father Myrc asked in a wavering voice, before muttering the *Pater Noster*.

"Came from in there," Farrier growled, and Tuck knew the young man was speaking in such a low tone so his voice wouldn't crack, and betray the terror he was feeling.

"Sounded like a man," said Amber quietly, and she too looked fearful now, which was perfectly understandable.

Surprisingly, it was Edward, hitherto silent and pale, who spoke up. "Go into the room," he said. "This is what we came for, isn't it?" He had thick, unkempt, sandy hair and bushy sideburns which combined to make him look somewhat comical, yet Tuck couldn't help admiring his courage.

"Agreed," said the friar. "Go on, Farrier. You wanted to see a ghost, and it sounds like there's one on the other side of that door."

Father Myrc's prayers grew louder but, as Farrier steeled himself to shove the door open, Simon and Eric shared a glance, and then both bolted back towards the front door without a word. Their footsteps could be heard pounding carelessly across the drawbridge and soon faded into the distance.

Lily laughed. "What a pair of cowards," she said.

"Aye," Tuck said, pulling his cudgel out of his belt, but silently wondering if the fleeing men had the right idea.

There came another low moan from the other room and Tuck's natural instincts came to the fore. Someone, either a living or a dead man, needed help, surely. People didn't normally groan like that unless they were injured or otherwise in trouble.

"Go on, Farrier", said the friar, nodding his head. "Amber, you and Lily get back behind me and Edward."

As the door was pushed slowly open by Farrier, the most horrific scream filled the hallway and seemed to make the crumbling old structure vibrate from floor to rotting rafters.

The hitherto stoic Edward decided that was enough for one night, and, like the other two frightened villagers before him, he turned and made for the front door as fast as possible. As he reached the drawbridge, he lost his footing for it was covered now in snow. Sobbing, Edward got up, rubbing his shoulder as if injured, then stumbled away without a backward glance.

Lily, perhaps recognising this as her own final chance to escape, went after him, throwing an apologetic glance at Amber as she ran, speedily but carefully, over the snowy drawbridge.

Father Myrc had finally stopped praying but his face was deathly pale and he tapped Tuck on the shoulder. "I had better go after Lily," he said. "We can't have a girl running around the countryside without a guardian." With that, he hurried away, his shouts of, "Lily! Wait on me!" fading into the distance.

Friar Tuck rolled his eyes. He was done with being careful. Someone was living here – the smell of the recently extinguished fire proved it. The stories of lights being seen within the house, of pained cries, and dark, hooded figures walking through the marshes towards the drawbridge, it all made sense now.

"Move, Farrier," he said, pushing past the terrified young man and stepping into the room where the groans and screams were emanating from. "That's no ghost – it's a man, and he needs help."

His words were cut off as something struck him on the top of his head and his legs gave way.

"Tuck!" Farrier couldn't tell what had happened for his eyes had been searching the far corners of the room and the lamps he and Amber held seemed to do nothing more than cast confusing shadows on the walls. "What's happening, Tuck?"

"Look out," cried Amber, and then Farrier too was on the ground, as the iron poker that had struck the friar now hit the younger man in the face with a sickening crack.

Amber stared at the downed men, wishing desperately that Little John was with her. She tried to control the shaking in her hands so that the oil lamp wouldn't fall from her grasp, for it would surely be much worse to be left alone in this room with the darkness and whatever had done for Tuck and Farrier.

She shrank back then, as a figure came into view. A tall, hooded shape, with, terrifyingly, no face. As she stared at the apparition, however, a hand reached up and pulled what looked like a sack over it's head, revealing a man's features. He had unruly hair and a grizzled beard and, at first glance she thought it was John before she noticed the raw, recently burned skin on his face and the realisation hit her.

"You're the fake bailiff," she managed to gasp.

"Fake?" The man's voice was a low growl and his eyes flashed in the gloom as if he was angered by her description of him. "I do better work than any of those fools granted powers by the sheriff. I collect unpaid fines, and bring justice to scum that deserve it. Fake?" He spat on the floor, the white spittle landing on Farrier's back. "I don't need authority from Sir Henry de Faucumberg – God chose me as his instrument of the law."

Amber glanced down at the two prone men and rage flooded her too. Farrier was a pleasant young man who wanted only to investigate a haunted house, and Tuck was one of her oldest, closest friends. "You're a murderer," she hissed, raising the dagger that was in her right hand. "And my husband will see you hang for your crimes."

The man stared at her for a moment, and then recognition dawned on his face. "You're John Little's wife."

"I am—"

He lashed out with the poker, striking Amber's wrist. A terrific pain lanced along her arm and she dropped her dagger, screaming and fearing bones had been broken. Before she could do anything else the man was upon her, hands around her throat, squeezing, forcing her down onto her knees.

As she began to lose consciousness, she saw her attacker smiling, teeth bared viciously.

"Your husband was an outlaw," he was saying. "He must face justice, as all the others before him. And you're going to bring him right to us."

Amber hammered her uninjured arm against the squeezing hands but it was hopeless and as darkness overcame her she could only think, *Us? Then there is another one of these maniacs. Oh, God help you, John!*

# CHAPTER SIXTEEN

It started with a low growl. One of the dogs made the rumbling sound not long after midnight and, with the crackling of the low fire being the only other sound in Will Scarlet's house, everyone heard it, apart from little Blase, and came instantly alert.

The toddler was fast asleep in the bed chamber with Elspeth but neither Will nor John made any attempt to silence the growling dog. Instead, they watched the beast with hands gripping their sheathed swords, ready to move at any moment. Neither man had heard anything from outside, but, as they looked on, the hackles on the hound's back rose, and then the other dog growled too.

Still, Will and John remained seated, senses straining, not wanting to disturb Blase's rest simply because the dogs had caught the scent of a fox passing by on its hunt for food.

Still growling, the first dog got up and padded across to stand beside Will's stool, staring fixedly at the front door.

"Good boy, Holdfast," said Scarlet, touching the dog's back reassuringly. This animal was the larger of the pair, with a black coat and muscular limbs. It was also, usually, less skittish than the other, a little brown terrier named Mite, so the fact that its hackles were raised was a sure sign something was off.

Now Mite gave a bark, not loud, but enough to be heard, and it too was eyeing the front door as if it expected someone to come through it.

"I've had enough of this waiting," Scarlet muttered, standing up and nodding to John. "Someone's out there, doing God knows what. We should go and find them."

John was always up for a fight, but he looked towards the bed chamber, worried that leaving Will's wife and son alone, undefended, was the best course of action.

"We won't go far," Will said softly, reading his friend's thoughts. "But we can't just sit here. The bastard might be setting fire to the roof right now!"

"He's right, John." Elspeth's melodious voice floated out of the adjoining room, but, before she could say anything else, Mite barked loudly at the door and ran towards it, sniffing at the gap beneath. This set off Holdfast, and his deeper bark filled the house in a quite disturbing manner.

"Go!" Elspeth called, cuddling Blase protectively as the lad asked in a sleepy, frightened tone what was happening.

"All right," Will agreed, heading for the door and throwing back the heavy bolt. "Lock this behind us though, and don't open it unless you know it's me!"

They went outside then, John holding onto Mite's leash while Will took the larger Holdfast. Both dogs were barking, snouts pointed in the same direction – east. Neither man carried a lamp so it was too dark to see if anyone was there, and Will decided to make a circuit of his house, reassured by the thump from inside as Elspeth pushed the bolt back into place.

"You go that way," he said to John, pointing to the left. "I'll go this way. Meet back here unless you see someone."

There were no jokes, no glib comments about chasing foxes or even ghosts – both men were on edge, the blood pounding in their veins, swords held ready to strike. God help anyone they met out here.

As Will rounded the first corner Holdfast stopped straining on his leash and bent to sniff at something. As Will's eyes adjusted to the gloom he stared down, trying to see what was there and finally realised it was a chunk of raw, pink meat. Why would there be meat lying outside his house?

"Back, boy!" he shouted, pulling hard on the leash as Holdfast sniffed warily at the morsel. *It's poisoned*, Will thought, kicking the meat as hard as he could, sending it flying away into the darkness. His fear had transferred to the dog, who made no attempt to go after the food and, instead, raised his head and began sniffing once more, searching for whoever was out there in the night.

"Will! Watch out, there's poisoned meat—"

John's voice carried over the house and Will called back to let him know he'd found it and to be on the lookout for more.

Suddenly Mite's yelping grew more ferocious, the thin, almost piping sound combining with Holdfast's more frightening, booming, bark.

"You see anyone, John?"

"No!"

Will continued to walk forward in the direction Holdfast was leading him, but he could tell this was pointless. Whoever had left the poisoned meat was still somewhere nearby, unless the dogs really were scenting a fox or similar nocturnal animal, but there was little chance of them catching anyone with the dogs giving away their position so loudly.

Leaning down, Will undid the leash around Holdfast's neck and muttered in the hound's ear, "Go get him, boy." Then, as the powerful dog raced away into the darkness, Will shouted to John, "Let the dog off! They can lead us to the bastard."

Moments later Mite's frantic, high-pitched bark could be heard, lowering in volume as the little terrier followed Holdfast into the night. They were moving east, away from the house, and Will glanced back over his shoulder, loath to leave his family behind, but then there came a new sound, of a man shouting in the field ahead.

John's great, pounding footsteps thundered in the darkness then and Will, praying to God to protect Elspeth and Blase, also sprinted towards the barking and shouting. As he ran it became clear the dogs had found their quarry, for the barking became even more aggressive but remained in the one position now as the man they'd found shouted, "Get back! Back, you bastards!"

"Take him alive, Will," John called, but Scarlet wasn't listening to his friend. He heard Holdfast snarl, then the man scream, and then, as Mite's barking became muffled as if she'd caught hold of something in her small but powerful jaws, there was a terrible squeal.

"No," Will gasped, forcing his legs to carry him faster, lungs burning as he finally caught up with the dogs and his harsh breathing turned to a sob. "No!"

Holdfast was on the ground, unmoving, a long, deep gash in her flank, as Mite courageously, and furiously, tried to tear apart the trousers of the man who was standing in the field, eyes wide in fright, sword in hand.

John reached them first, and, before the stunned man could defend himself, the bailiff's blade flashed in the darkness, striking the stranger's blade with a ringing clatter, and then John's fist hammered into his face. The man collapsed instantly, unconscious or dazed, and little Mite ran to attack his neck and face. John had to push the enraged dog away with his foot before hurriedly sheathing his weapon and reattaching the leash to Mite, who nipped at his hands in outrage before he finally got her under control.

Will knelt, staring at the groaning man's face without recognition – it truly was a stranger. And then he turned his attention to Holdfast, pressing his hand against her ribs as tears filled his eyes.

He cursed himself, wondering how a man like him could have become so attached to a stupid dog in the few weeks he'd owned the animal, and wishing he'd not been so quick to let Holdfast off the leash. It was his fault she was dead.

"You recognise him?" John asked, huffing loudly as he tried to catch his breath, apparently unaware of Will's anguish.

"No," Scarlet gasped, also breathless but with emotion as much as from running. "But he's…" His voice trailed off and he stared at Holdfast, wondering if he was imagining things. Had his hand moved on her ribs? It had! The dog was still breathing, despite the injury to her side.

"What in God's name are you doing?" John demanded, as Will pulled took out his knife and used it to cut a long piece from their unconscious attacker's cloak. Then, neck muscles straining, he tore the material, so he was left holding a long strip. Will carefully bandaged Holdfast's torso with it, talking softly to her the whole time as the giant bailiff looked on. When he was finished, he took the dog in his arms, stood up, and started the walk back to his house.

"Use the leash to tie that whoreson's hands," he called over his shoulder to John. "And, when he wakes up, bring him to the house. If you haven't broken his neck with that punch, he'll soon be wishing you had."

# CHAPTER SEVENTEEN

Adam Baxter thought of himself as a good man. A moral man, who worked hard every day as a carpenter, visited church on a Sunday, and tried to be a good friend to his childhood companion, Geoffrey. Hadn't they been doing good work lately? he asked himself as he carried John Little's wife through the marshes. If the real bailiffs wouldn't deal with outlaws and the dregs of society, well they would do it instead.

"Don't try to escape," he snarled at Amber as she came to just as they finally reached one of the manor's outbuildings. This one was in rather better condition than the other structures dotted about the place, with sturdy new doors and a lock recently fitted by Baxter himself. To stop anyone prying into this particular structure, two skulls, belonging to a sheep and a goat, had been attached above the doors. On the entrance itself, he'd painted a diagram consisting of a rectangle with an inverted cross and the letters *er, hx, xh* and *hx* at the corners. In the centre were the letters *h,d,n* and *d* running down on either side of the cross.

He had no idea what any of it meant, it was just something he'd found scratched into the old walls of a church he'd been helping to renovate years before. Clearly it was some magical spell, probably to stop thieves or something, and, to Adam, it looked incredibly sinister. He knew it, and the animal skulls, would deter any nosy villagers from breaking into the building.

If they had taken the time to smash open the lock they'd not have found any hoarded gold, as Amber saw when her captor put her down on the ground and pulled open the door to reveal merely a horse. It looked quite content and snorted softly as its master stroked its neck and led it out into the cold air.

"Get up," Adam said to his prisoner and, when she failed to move, he slapped her on the back of the head and roughly pushed her up onto the horse's back, telling her he'd bind her limbs and throw her over the saddle like a sack of grain if she didn't co-operate. Then, holding the reins so she wouldn't try to ride off, he locked the doors and hauled himself up behind her.

"Where are you taking me?" Amber asked, and her voice was stronger than Adam had expected given her treatment so far.

"Never you mind," he replied. "I've no desire to harm you. I'm in the business of dealing out justice, not hurting innocent women. But you've got in my way, and now I've a chance to deal with one of the biggest criminals in England."

The woman barked, something halfway between a laugh and a sob. "You mean my husband?" She shook her head. "He'll find you, and he'll make sure you never do anything like this again. Why d'you think everyone knows his name? Because he's kind and gentle?"

She laughed again and Adam gritted his teeth. He did know all the stories about John and his companions in Robin Hood's gang. They'd been a dangerous group right enough, killing and torturing any who crossed their path. Yet, somehow, the people of Yorkshire loved them! He'd been a youngster when the gang was operating so he couldn't really remember much about the time, but, to him, they'd been outlaws and should have faced justice. Yet they'd all been pardoned, and now this woman's husband was a lawman himself!

It was *not* just. Not to Adam's mind at least. No doubt they'd used some of the money they'd stolen from poor merchants and clergymen to bribe the sheriff and his lackeys, and been left to live their lives as free men.

Well, Adam's friend Geoffrey would hopefully deal with the one called Will Scaflock this very night, and then, when John Little came looking for his wife, he'd get his comeuppance.

"No-one knows who I am, apart from you, but I hope your man does come to find me," growled the would-be bailiff. "For he'll get a nice surprise when he comes into my house." Then it was his turn to laugh grimly as they galloped towards his home village of Kirkthorpe.

It didn't take that long to reach the place and, similarly to his stable at the manor, Adam had stables that were set a short distance away from the main village street, so he and his friend could come and go without anyone noting their nocturnal movements.

"Come on," he muttered to Amber, eyes scanning the trees that lay between them and the houses they were heading towards. "And don't make any noise or I'll kill you. You know I've already killed people, so don't think I won't do it." He held her by the hair and gave it a tug as he spoke to emphasise his point. He did not want to harm her just yet, but he wouldn't let her think he was soft either.

They saw no one in the street as they made for their destination. Everyone was safely indoors on this freezing night and, soon enough, so were Adam and his prisoner.

"Do you really think it's clever to bring me to your own home?" Amber asked once they were sitting eyeing one another in the small house and only the noise of a great pig snoring in the sty beside the house penetrated the silence.

Adam's burned lip curled at one side and his eyes twinkled with amusement. "But this isn't my home," he said. "My house is near the bottom of the street and, like I said earlier, when your man goes in there to search for me, he'll find a nice surprise waiting for him."

"What surprise?" Amber demanded, moving to stand up but relaxing again when Adam pulled out a long knife and waved it at her warningly.

He didn't reply though, just stared at her until she turned away, expression tight with fear and expectation.

# CHAPTER EIGHTEEN

"What's wrong with Holdfast?" Blase was not yet three years old but his speech was good and, as the little boy stood in the door of the bedchamber and watched Will tending to the injured dog, Elspeth tried to reassure him.

"He's been hurt, my lamb," she said, scooping up the boy and cuddling him tightly. Like her husband, she too had tears in her eyes at the sight of the wounded dog, but she did not want their son to see anything that might happen during the rest of the night. The dog might die, but, from the black expression on Scarlet's face, so too might the man they'd taken prisoner.

"Come back to bed," Elspeth said, and took the unprotesting child into the bedchamber, giving John a final, worried look, before closing the door and leaving the men to finish their business. Whatever that might be. In the few years they'd been together Will had never raised a hand to her – in fact, he was the kindest, most loving man she could have wished to marry. But she knew there was a dark side to him, for she'd heard all the stories about him, often from his own mouth. Sometimes, before they fell asleep, Will would tell her about the family he'd had before, and the things he'd done to avenge their deaths, and they would both cry.

She feared what he might do to the man in their house now. Holdfast might only be a dog, but would Will see it like that? There was a good chance the man was an outlaw, a wolf's head, and, as such, it would be quite legal for Will to kill him. But she did not want someone killed in their home, and she did not want Will to add to the grim burden he carried with him every day – he had enough to come to terms with as it was.

Hopefully Little John would look after them – he was good at that, Elspeth thought with a sad smile.

And then something happened that put all thoughts of mercy from her mind, and she'd have gladly tortured their captive herself if the need arose: Friar Tuck arrived.

Mite heard the approaching hoofbeats before the rest of them again, setting up a terrific yammering which sent John out into the night, sword raised, ready to annihilate this new threat to their safety. Elspeth appeared at his side, holding a long knife, and she looked just as ready to murder as her husband for this had been a long, trying night already and she'd had enough of it.

Will was still tending to Holdfast's injury and did not want to leave her until he'd finished cleaning, stitching and applying a fresh, proper bandage to the wound. He could tell from the sound it was only one rider on the way and he had little doubt John could deal with a single enemy, no matter who it was.

Their prisoner lay on the floor of the house, securely tied, awake but silently watching everything that was happening. Will spotted a flicker of hope in his eyes when he heard the drumming hooves, but it quickly faded as they heard the bailiff outside calling, "Tuck! What the hell are you doing here in the middle of the night?"

The friar practically fell out of the saddle, landing unsteadily and needing to hold the reins to stop himself from collapsing.

John's sword was sheathed in a moment and he ran to support his friend, who looked dazed, pale, and not at all healthy. His tonsured head was bleeding, and, from the amount on his crown and face it had clearly been going for some time.

"God's bollocks," John breathed, taking in the sorry sight and helping Tuck towards the house as Elspeth quickly led the horse to the stables for it had begun snowing again and she didn't want the animal to freeze. Mite followed her protectively and she smiled at the dog. "I'm glad you're here to look after us," she said. "Since it looks like the night's excitement isn't over yet."

Expertly, she dealt with the horse, making sure it was comfortable and secure before locking the stable and running through the snow back to the house, Mite guarding her every step. She was glad to get the door closed and let the warmth from the banked fire seep into her bones. Blase was wide awake again and sitting on a stool at the table with a blanket wrapped about him. He seemed to be enjoying himself, unlike everyone else gathered in the farmhouse. It was amazing how resilient children could be. Elspeth took a seat beside him and hugged him as she waited to find out why Tuck was there.

The friar was dazed and looked like he might even vomit at one point, but Will, who had finished bandaging Holdfast by now, fetched fresh water and used his healing skills to deal with Tuck. The blood was wiped from the friar's crown and John shuddered as he saw the egg-sized swelling there.

Still the bailiff had not begun to suspect what was wrong but, as he took in the extent of Tuck's injury, and the fact he'd ridden to them in such a state, a cold chill settled upon John and it wasn't a result of the snow falling outside.

"Where's Amber?" he demanded, fear for his beloved wife's welfare overriding his concern for Tuck's safety. "What's happened?"

The friar was still not his usual self, but Will's ministrations, and the blazing fire, had at least brought some colour back to his cheeks. He breathed heavily, labouring, and despite his anxiety John found a mug of ale and held it to his friend's lips that he might swallow some. Mite did her bit too, lying by Tuck's side as if lending him some of her own little body's heat. The injured man's fingers stroked her smooth coat almost instinctively, something John took as a good sign.

After what seemed like an age, the friar eventually seemed to revive and remember where he was, but, as he met John's gaze, a wave of fear washed over the bailiff.

"Amber's been taken," Tuck said, wincing as he spoke. "We were attacked in the manor house. I was knocked out. So was Farrier." He groaned and bent his head as pain lanced through his damaged skull. "When I came to, Amber was not there, and neither was our attacker. I helped Farrier back to town then headed here."

John and Will looked at one another, stunned by this terrible turn of events. What was going on in their quiet village, by God?

"Someone's been living in the old house," Tuck continued, taking the ale mug from John and sipping from it in hopes of the liquid easing some of his pain.

"What?" John asked, shaking his head in confusion. "Who would choose to live in such a place?"

"An outlaw," said Will. "Like William Bywater."

John nodded, mind racing as he tried to come to terms with what was going on and decide what to do next.

"We're no outlaws."

The words were spoken by the prisoner in the corner, who'd been almost forgotten in all the latest excitement. Everyone turned in his direction now, puzzled by the unexpected and cryptic remark.

"What?" Will demanded, standing up rather stiffly after kneeling to minister to first Holdfast, and then Tuck.

"We're no outlaws," the captive repeated, lip curling in disdain, but, seeing only confusion on the faces of those looking at him, he said, "We might not have the sheriff's authority, but we're as much bailiffs as you, John Little."

Will stepped across to stand over the man and shook his head. "Are you saying you, and some accomplice, have been going about Yorkshire assaulting folk? Murdering them? Setting alight to their homes? That was all you, was it? And you've been hiding out in the old manor house in the marsh?"

Now it seemed their prisoner was regretting his outburst, and he turned his eyes to the floor, clenching his jaw before a sudden, sharp pain reminded him of John's earlier punch.

"Answer him!" Little John was in no mood to mess about now that he knew Amber was in danger and possibly being killed at that very moment. He ran to the prisoner, bent his knees, and lifted the man by the front of his cloak right up so his feet drummed against the wall and his face was filled with terror.

"Aye," the prisoner gasped, eyes bulging. "We're not living in the ruined house, we have our own homes in—" He broke off, no doubt unwilling to give too much away. "We've just been using it as a base, and to store the money we've taken from people in fines."

"Fines?" John demanded, and his fury seemed hotter than the fire in the hearth beside them. "Where's my wife, you piece of shit? Where's your mate taken her? Speak, or so help me God, I'll smash your head right through this wall!"

Behind them, Elspeth took Blase by the hand and led him quickly into the bedchamber again. The boy didn't seem frightened or upset, just surprised, for he only knew Little John as a big, friendly giant who played with him and acted silly to make him laugh. *This* version of Little John was something the boy had never seen before, and Elspeth did not really want him to witness it.

Although, truth be told, if Blase hadn't been there, Elspeth would have been right by John's side seeking answers, for Amber was her friend and she was terribly afraid for her. These so-called bailiffs were known murderers after all, and they seemed to have little respect for women.

"I don't know!" the prisoner shouted desperately, and Will tapped John's arm, nodding to let him know he should put the man down. The bailiff did so, dropping him unceremoniously and the captive, who still had his hands bound behind his back, collapsed in a heap, striking his face against the floor with a thump.

His ordeal was not over, however.

Will knelt next to him and drew out a knife, which he held in front of the prisoner's face. "You see this? Well, you're a wolf's head, you're outside the law, and that means we can do whatever we like to you."

The man's lower lip trembled but he didn't reply, other than to look beseechingly at Tuck, but the friar merely stared back coldly.

"What I'm going to do," said Will in a low, dangerous voice, "is this: I'm going to gag your mouth so my boy can't hear you screaming, and then I'm going to cut your fingers off, one by one, until you tell us where John's wife is. You understand?" As he spoke, he was using the knife to cut off a strip of the captive's cloak, to be used as the gag he'd promised.

"I don't know where he's taken her, I swear by God and all his saints," the prisoner sobbed, utterly terrified now, for there were rumours that Will Scarlet had once broken into a man's house, tied him to a chair, and then chopped off his fingers. Looking into his eyes now, the prisoner could quite believe the tale was true.

"Who's 'he' anyway?" Tuck asked. "His name?"

The man stared at him, then, noticing Will had stopped moving, said, "Adam Baxter. I'm Geoffrey Comber. We're both from Kirkthorpe."

That was a village just a few miles from Wakefield but John, staring at the prisoner, did not recognise him. "Where would Adam have taken my wife? Is there somewhere, other than your little hideout, where he'd feel safe? Where he'd go to meet you after this night's work? Think carefully," he warned. "Because if you don't help us, Will taking your fingers off with his knife will seem like heaven by the time I've finished with you."

"I don't know!" the man wailed. "We always just went to the old house, because we didn't think anyone would be brave enough to come there, what with all the ghost stories about the place."

"There must be somewhere," John persisted. "Somewhere your friend would feel safe going to." He gestured vaguely with a nod of his chin to the window. "It's snowing outside. He'll want to go somewhere warm, right? But he's got my wife as a prisoner, so he'll need to go someplace no one'll disturb him."

Geoffrey frowned, forehead creasing as he desperately tried to give these madmen a suitable answer to their questions. He had no thoughts of sparing his accomplice – all he wanted was to save his own skin. "The only place I can think of, would be his own home. His ma died when he was young, and his da died last year, so Adam lives there alone. He's not married or anything."

"Where is it?" John demanded, checking his sword was sheathed and pulling the cord around his cloak as he made ready to ride.

Again, Geoffrey paused to think, to visualise Kirkthorpe in his mind, and then he said, "It's the fifth house along the main street. Quite a big house, set a little way back from the road."

Little John took this in, and then he tilted his head thoughtfully, almost like one of Will's dogs. "I know that house," he said. "It belonged to a forester. Good man. Helped me out a few times in my work."

"That's right," Geoffrey agreed. "That was Adam's da, Alexander. Look, we're not bad men. We just wanted to bring justice to people who deserved it. I admit, we might have got a bit carried away but...Please don't hurt Adam."

His words fell on deaf ears.

"Right, I'm going to Kirkthorpe," John growled, looking at Will and then Tuck. "Anyone want to come with me?"

"I can't," the friar replied sadly, touching his shaved, injured scalp gingerly. "But I'm sure I'll be able to keep him in check, with Elspeth to help," he waved a hand at the prisoner. "Just check his bonds before you go. Maybe tie his feet as well."

This was hastily, but carefully done, and then, with hurried goodbyes, John and Will ran to fetch their horses, Elspeth bolting the door behind them against the flurries of snow and unlikely possibility of further threats to the household.

As they galloped away, Tuck gladly accepted another drink from Elspeth who was greatly relieved to see the friar's cheeks their usual rosy red rather than the deathly white they'd been earlier.

Incredibly, little Blase had gone back to sleep despite all the uproar, so Elspeth tucked him into bed with a thick woollen blanket and then came over to join the friar in guarding their prisoner.

"Can I have some of that ale?" Geoffrey asked, noting Elspeth's tenderness in dealing with both Tuck and her child. "Maybe a crust of bread too, my guts are rumbling here." If he thought she was a soft touch, however, he was soon disabused of the idea, as her eyes blazed and she turned to him.

"You'll get nothing from me, except a slap across the face, wolf's head, if you don't shut your mouth!" She shook a fist at him. "If anything happens to my friend, you'll be sorry."

The three of them sat in silence then, Tuck and Elspeth praying that everything would turn out well although, while they didn't want to admit it to themselves, things looked very bad for Little John's wife.

It was going to be a long night. With that in mind, Tuck turned to Geoffrey and said, "Well, why don't you tell us what you've been up to, lad? What made you think you could pretend to be a bailiff?"

The prisoner glared at him sullenly for a time, but then, like most people, the opportunity to talk about himself and his beliefs overcame any reticence, and he began telling his story.

# CHAPTER NINETEEN

Their horses' hooves churned the snow as they headed for Kirkthorpe, and John was mindful of the fact that, although time was of the essence, if one of their mounts was injured it would be disastrous. So they moved fast, but not recklessly so, praying as they went that this was indeed the right way and Amber wasn't being carried off in the opposite direction.

Or worse, already beyond their help…

Will knew what it was to lose a wife to a madman's brutal actions, and he felt John's anxiety almost as keenly as the big bailiff. They did not converse as they rode, but the village was not too far from Will's house and, once they were on the main road, the miles passed quickly. Soon enough they saw the squat black shapes of houses and caught the scent of smoke from banked fires rising into the sky, guiding them to their destination. At this time of year most homes kept their fire burning throughout the night if possible, to keep the home as cosy as safely possible and so there was something warm – broth or pottage – readily available to keep the occupants' bellies filled.

Of course, the lack of a fire could also be suggestive. As John led the way into the village they dismounted and, pegging their horses to the ground, moved stealthily towards the fifth house on the left. There was no sweet-smelling woodsmoke emanating from the chimney-hole in the thatched roof.

"If he's there, he's not been home for long," Will muttered. "On a night like this the first thing a man does when he gets in is build the fire and warm some ale."

"Unless he's too busy," John said in a dull voice, as if he didn't want to think about what might make the house's occupants too busy to get a fire going.

Will nodded but offered no platitudes. They were not wanted or needed. Instead, he drew his sword and moved towards the house in a crouch, eyes scanning the building as he went, taking in the positions of the door and windows and listening for signs of danger.

John came at his back, also with blade drawn, and the pair moved silently through the snow. Will went to the left, while John went right, but they came together at the door in the front of the house. There was no other way in, and the windows were all tightly shuttered.

Unlike the other dwellings they could see, this house had not been decorated with holly, ivy and other cheery winter greenery, making it seem even darker and less inviting to John and Will's eyes.

They stood and listened, shivering in the cold and trying to make sure their teeth didn't chatter and give them away for it was truly bitter. An owl hooted in the trees to the south but nothing else could be heard. The village seemed completely at peace.

Will nodded to his friend and stepped in front of the door, ready to kick it open, but John shook his head.

"What's wrong?" Will asked, leaning in close so his voice didn't carry. "We need to get in there. Now."

"Something's off," John said. "Look at the snow." He pointed the tip of his sword at the ground. Their footsteps could be seen clearly in the moonlight for the snow had stopped a little while ago and the clouds had parted, but there were no other prints.

Will frowned and then went to check in the stable which stood close to the house. They'd already looked inside when they first arrived, but the significance of what he was seeing now struck Will. "It's empty," he said.

John nodded. "No one's come here in the past few hours."

"Geoffrey lied to us," Will growled. "He sent us here so his mate could escape! Shit!"

"Maybe not," John said, patting the air with his palm to tell his companion to keep his voice down. "I think Geoffrey was too frightened to lie."

"Then where's his mate? And where's Amber?"

John shook his head. "I don't know, but we might as well check in here and see if there's any clues that might help us find them." With that he ran at the door, his enormous bulk crashing against it and completely shattering the frame which attached it to the wall.

They walked into the house as a dog started barking in the next dwelling along the street. Adam Baxter's home had two rooms: the largest one which they were standing in now, with a hearth, and a table and all the things used for daily living; and a second, smaller room which must be the bedchamber.

John looked about, but it was pitch black and he was loath to waste time lighting the fire for it would surely be time wasted – there was clearly no one there.

"What's happening?" A man appeared in the ruined front doorway, snarling dog by his side but secured by a leash. "Who the hell are you two?"

In his hand he carried a lantern and, holding it into the house he took in the sight of the two big men and blanched, clearly regretting his decision to come and investigate what was happening at his neighbour's house.

"I'm John Little," said John. "Bailiff. We're looking for the man who lives here, you've nothing to fear from us."

"Unless…" Will growled. "You *are* the man who lives here."

"What? No!" The villager stepped back fearfully, shaking his head. "I live in the house next door. I just came to see what the dog was barking at. You're looking for Adam. Is he not home?"

"Shine your candle in here," John commanded, gesturing with his hand, and the man obeyed, the small flame doing just enough to let them get a proper look about.

The main room was sparsely furnished, and the one storage chest only contained some clothes and a thick blanket. There was a decent quality silver spoon and knife set on the table, and a well-made iron cauldron although there was no food in it, just some greasy remnants. A pot of honey lay out and John noted the finger marks in it, as if someone had been smearing it on themselves. As a soothing balm for a burned face, perhaps.

The bailiff's eyes were drawn towards the bedchamber then, and Will had the same idea for he was walking towards the smaller room now.

Still, something nagged at John. Something here wasn't quite right. This house, its contents, it all looked quite normal, but the bailiff had a nagging feeling that they were in danger, which was absurd, as they were clearly alone.

So, why did he feel like they were in grave danger?

\* \* \*

Adam walked to the table in the corner of the room and filled a cup from the jug of ale that was kept there. He sipped it while looking thoughtfully at his prisoner. Should he bother tying her up? That would mean finding some rope or tearing a blanket or something into strips and, honestly, after everything that had been happening that night, he couldn't be bothered. The woman was no trouble, for she knew he'd kill her in an instant if she pushed him too far.

"D'you want some ale?" he asked, holding out the cup to her.

Rather than reply to his question she asked one of her own. "Why are you pretending to be a bailiff?"

It was something he'd thought about a lot recently, for his work as a 'lawman' had become the most important thing in his life.

"I'm a carpenter," he said. "My father was a forester, and his father was a baker. All good, important jobs. But," he took another drink and arched his back for it felt stiff after their ride, "I've been fleeced by people over the years. People I've done work for, who never bothered paying me. My grandfather was always complaining about folk stealing his cakes too." He shook his head and felt the familiar rage building inside. "I hate thieves," he growled. "So, it was always my wish to be a bailiff, or a reeve, or a beadle."

"Why didn't you become one then?" Amber asked.

Adam stared at her. "It's hard for someone like me to get a job like that," he said, and it was true. He'd never been taught to read or write, and he wasn't good with numbers, all of which were necessary for a bailiff. "And the steward was no friend of mine, so he'd never give me the job. Last year though, someone stole a load of horseshoes from the farrier's workshop. The hue-and-cry was raised, and I chased after the thief. Me and my friend, Geoffrey, caught him and…" He paused, reliving that event with relish "He tried to fight us off, but we gave him the beating he deserved and held him down until others came to help and carted him off to face justice."

"You beat up a man and it made you feel important," Amber said coldly, but Adam didn't even notice the rebuke in her words. Or the disdain.

He nodded happily. "Aye, exactly. Catching that thief was the greatest thing I'd ever done, and the farrier's gratitude made it even better. Me and Geoffrey were seen as heroes! I knew then that I should be doing more things like that with my life, but I couldn't see how. You sure you don't want a drink?"

Amber shook her head so he refilled the cup himself, appreciating the glow spreading through his body from the ale and enjoying telling his story to his captive audience.

"Anyway, one day I was in the alehouse and I overheard someone talking about the ruined house in the marshes near Wakefield. They said there was a ghost there, of a dead nobleman who'd hidden treasure in the grounds and now haunted the place. People were terrified to go near the old house because of these stories, so it was falling to ruin." He went to the door and unlatched it, putting his head outside to listen for any sound of his fellow 'bailiff' returning. The street was silent however, apart from the barking of a dog further down the way, so, beginning to wonder if all was well with Geoffrey, he pushed the door over and returned to his tale. "I went to see the ruined house. Ghosts don't scare me, not really. I found that, aye, most of the building was dangerous but, being a carpenter, I was able to make some of it safe enough to use as a base. Somewhere to store the fines I'd be collecting from criminals. A place where no one would ever snoop about in."

"Until tonight."

He sighed. "Aye. Until you and your nosey mates came along. I thought you'd all run away when I made the loud groaning noises. Would have been better for everyone if you had! I suppose I won't be able to use the house as a base anymore, I'll have to find somewhere else."

"But what you're doing is, well," Amber considered her words carefully before saying, "outside the law."

"Maybe," Adam replied glibly. "But we only target criminals. They deserve what they get."

"The men you attacked tonight didn't deserve what they got! I don't deserve what you're doing now."

He shrugged. "It's unfortunate, but sometimes life isn't very fair. Me and Geoffrey have our work to do, and I won't let anyone stop us. We'll use you as bait to bring your man to us – dealing with a famous wolf's head like the infamous Little John will top everything we've done before."

"And then you'll kill me too," Amber said, and although she'd dealt with everything stoically so far Adam could hear the fear in her voice. She knew what would happen eventually. "But, like you say, my husband will be looking for me by now, and he'll not let you escape."

"I told you before," he smiled slyly. "This isn't my house, so even if your man somehow discovers who I am, he won't come here to find me. This is my friend Geoffrey's house. I'm just waiting for him to come back before we decide what to do next. He should be here any moment now and, with luck, he'll have taken care of another of your outlaw friends: Will Scaflock. Geoffrey's been scouting his farm for a couple of nights now."

Amber's eyes snapped up, as if his words had shocked her.

"What?" he demanded, unnerved by her look.

"I doubt your accomplice will be coming back here any time soon, then," she said viciously, taking obvious pleasure in her words. "Because Will and my husband are back in Wakefield waiting to catch him. In fact, if it wasn't against the Church's rules, I'd wager your friend is already dead!"

"You're lying," Adam replied, but his face had turned pale for the woman's smile had an unnerving conviction behind it.

"We'll see," she said. "But my guess is that it won't be your little companion coming here to find you any time soon – it'll be John and Will Scarlet. And then we'll see how tough you are."

"You're a lying bitch!" Adam jumped up, rage filling him as he realised his days acting as a bailiff – as someone important – might be coming to an end, probably along with his life. He grabbed her and they fell on the floor, his left hand grinding her face into the earth while he tried to bring out his knife from where he'd pushed it back into his belt.

Suddenly there was a terrific thump from somewhere nearby, so powerful that Adam felt it reverberating through the ground. A fierce joy flooded through him for he knew what the sound meant and, as he paused to bask in his triumph, Amber's elbow lashed out, smashing into his nose and sending him reeling backwards.

Rather than returning to the attack, though, Adam stood up, pressing his nose in a futile attempt to stop the blood flowing. "Your legendary John Little isn't so clever now," he spat at his prisoner gleefully, and then, knowing he had to get away as quickly as possible, he aimed one last kick at Amber's head and ran out into the night.

# CHAPTER TWENTY

As Scarlet stepped into the doorway to the bedchamber, John bellowed, "Will!" and launched himself across the room, dragging his friend backwards as there was a terrific crash, and dust billowed about the place, setting the hound barking and howling in alarm.

"By Christ," the neighbour shouted, falling out the front door as his dog tugged on the leash, hard enough to pull free and sprint off along the snowy street. "What's happening?"

"You all right, Will?" John demanded, ignoring the villager and bending to help his friend. Scarlet was uninjured, thankfully, but looked shocked as he took in the scene in the house.

The door frame which he'd just been about to pass through had collapsed, but not just with the weight of some wood – heavy stone bricks were scattered about the floor, with one particularly large, flat piece of stone in the centre of it all.

"What the—?"

"It was a trap," John said, and he grabbed Will by the sleeve, pulling him outside. "Come on. Let's get the hell out in case there's any more. Or in case the rest of the house comes down."

"A trap?" Will looked down at his leg, puzzled. "I *did* feel something, now you mention it. Like a wire pressing against my shin."

John nodded. "That must have been what triggered it all to come down."

They turned and, with the villager's lantern still casting its light on the scene, gazed at the rubble-filled house. Clearly, the bricks had been rigged to come down on top of anyone walking into the bedroom which, given the terrific weight of it all, would have been fatal for the person underneath.

"How did you know?" Will asked, quickly stepping back into the house to retrieve the sword that had fallen from his grasp when John struck him.

The bailiff nodded to the villager. "When he appeared with his candle, I noticed the door frame leading into the bedchamber. Two massive wooden beams."

They all looked and saw what he described.

"The wall between the two rooms is just a curtain. There isn't even a proper door there. So why the need for such a strong frame?"

"To support all that rubble," the neighbour whispered, horrified at what he'd just witnessed. "But why?"

Will spat on the icy ground. "Must have been worried the law would discover what he'd been up to and come looking for him. That lot" – he nodded at the fallen bricks – "would soon put a stop to anyone searching for him. For a while at least."

"Look," John said, turning to the local again. "We've wasted enough time here. Your fellow villager, Adam Baxter, is a wanted criminal. A wolf's head. And he's abducted my wife."

The astonished man's mouth dropped open and he gaped stupidly at the bailiff.

"We were told he'd be here," John gestured at the booby-trapped dwelling. "But he's bloody well not.

So, do you have any idea where else he might be hiding?"

The villager's mouth worked for a moment as he marshalled his thoughts and tried to take in everything that was being said to him. And then he shrugged apologetically. "I don't know," he admitted. "But he only has one friend: Geoffrey Comber. Maybe he's at his."

John and Will looked at one another. The suggestion made perfect sense, and it was all they had to go on now anyway.

"Where?" John demanded.

"Halfway up the road, there," the neighbour said, pointing. "The one with the pigs at the side."

John was already running, and Will followed, struggling to keep up with his friend's long strides.

This was their last chance – if Amber wasn't here, she was as good as dead.

There were no pigs wandering in the plot of land attached to the house the villager had indicated belonged to Geoffrey, but there was a large sty and an unmistakeable smell. This was the place, surely. A smaller house than Adam Baxter's, this one was circular and could only contain a single room.

John was no longer interested in being stealthy, or scouting around the house for signs of occupation – he simply ran to the door and booted it, hard. It swung open easily and he went inside with sword in hand.

Will was not quite so impetuous and ran around to the rear, smashing a hole in the shutters there with his sword's pommel and jumping through the window.

"Amber!"

John was kneeling on the hard, earthen floor, eyes straining in the gloom at the figure he held in his arms. It was dark, but even so Will could see the long, thick hair, and knew they'd found John's wife.

"Amber!" the bailiff said again, louder, a note of desperation in his voice. He wished he'd asked the villager with the candle to follow them now, for, without the benefit of light, his imagination was working furiously, filling his mind with images of what might have happened to Amber: a slashed throat? Stab wounds? A smashed skull? Bruises? "Please, Amber, wake up."

Will was looking around the house, wary of an attack from the man who'd brought Amber here, but there was no place to hide in such a small space, and no sign of any attacker.

"John?"

"Oh, God be praised, you're alive!"

"Yes, I'm..." Amber's voice was weak, filled with anxiety, but seemed strong enough. "I think I'm all right," she said. "But I'm so cold." She cried out then, pain from her injured wrist reminding her that Adam had struck her with the poker.

Will immediately hastened to the hearth, setting to work with the flint and steel that were in his own pouch and soon had a fire going. They were even able to close the door over since it had been unlatched when John kicked it open and remained undamaged. It was snowing outside again, and the wind had picked up, so they were all glad when the fire was blazing and the room started to warm up.

John used the light to examine Amber for wounds but she was surprisingly well, other than her wrist, which he quickly strapped up using wood and cloth he found in the house, and bruising to her head and neck.

"Praise God," the bailiff murmured, kissing his wife as he held her tightly. "I feared that madman would kill you."

"He would have, eventually," Amber said, head pressed against John's shoulder. "He was waiting for some friend, Geoffrey, to come back here first. Then the two of them were going to use me as bait to kill you."

"Where did he go?" Will asked, still eyeing the gap in the shutters in case her abductor returned.

"We heard the dog barking down the street and a loud thumping and crashing," Amber said, lifting her head. "He was attacking me at the time, so when he was distracted by the noise I elbowed him in the face. Got the bastard right on the nose." She smiled in grim satisfaction at the memory of Adam's cry of pain and the feel of her bone connecting with his face.

"That's my girl," John said, hugging her proudly.

"He was angry about it though, kicked me, I think. I don't remember anything after that until you came in and found me on the floor."

Will cursed, slamming his hand against the wall in frustration. "He's off again, then, and this time we have no idea where to. We'll never find him now."

John sighed, but he was smiling. "Maybe so," he agreed. "But at least we're all safe, and we still have Geoffrey as a prisoner. He might be able to help us find his friend again, if he thinks it'll save his own skin."

Will frowned. "Look, John," he said. "I know you're glad Amber's safe. So am I. But we can't just let this arsehole escape. Who knows what he'll do next, or who he'll hurt? We'll never sleep well again, until we know he's been dealt with, and now's our best chance."

"How?" John asked, clearly reluctant to leave his wife's side after her ordeal.

"Look," Will said, pushing open one of the shutters to reveal the snow drifting down outside. "He'll be leaving tracks wherever he's going. We can follow him."

John still wasn't convinced. "But we don't even know where to start! He could have gone in any direction."

Just then there was a knocking sound and they all started, Will and John drawing their swords and shifting into defensive stances instinctively. The door opened slowly though, to reveal the villager they'd spoken with earlier and Will snorted with relieved laughter.

"I'm sorry to disturb you," said the man, looking at Amber with great surprise and interest and John knew the villager would be straight off to tell everyone about this fresh new piece of gossip as soon as he'd said his piece.

"What's wrong?" the bailiff asked not unkindly.

"Well, it's Adam," the man said. "You know, the lad you're looking for?"

"What about him," demanded Will, coming across and sticking his head out the door to look up and down the street.

"He's ridden off on one of your horses."

This revelation brought the obvious reaction, as both John and Will ran into the street, staring down at where they'd left their mounts.

"Come on, John," said Will, already heading back towards the house with the collapsing doorframe. "Now we know where he started, and his tracks will let us follow him."

"We've only one horse!" John argued. "And I'm not leaving Amber alone, not after what's happened. The bastard might be leading us away, only to come back when we're off looking for him."

"We'll take care of her," the villager said, and he gestured towards the people who'd come from their own houses to see what all the fuss was about.

"Do you have another horse we can borrow?" Will asked.

"Aye," a man replied, grinning, absolutely thrilled by the night's entertainment. "I've got some in my stables, as long as you bring it back safely."

John was still shaking his head adamantly. "I'm not leaving Amber," he said, but his wife interrupted him somewhat irritably. Now that she'd warmed up she was back to her old self.

"I'm not a child, John," she said. "I managed to break the bastard's nose, didn't I? Besides, you won't be leaving me here – I'm coming with you. I want to see him caught just as much as anyone. More!"

"What's happening?" A middle-aged, portly man with an officious air pushed his way to the front of the crowd and stood looking up at the towering figure of Little John. "Why are you men chasing Adam Baxter? I'm the headman here, and I demand to know."

John clenched his teeth, in no mood for further delays, but he could see the rest of the villagers expected an answer too. Even if they didn't have any great friendship with Adam, he was still one of them – a Kirkthorpe man.

"Him and his friend, Geoffrey, are the ones who've been going about pretending to be bailiffs. Stealing, burning property, murdering, abducting..."

"Good!"

John and Will both rounded on the man who'd called out. He looked to be in about his mid-sixties and his deeply lined face was set in a grimace of approval.

"Good?"

The old man nodded at Will.

"Aye. Good. It's about time someone stood up against all the lawlessness in Yorkshire. It's a bloody disgrace what goes on around here."

"Are you stupid?" John demanded. "Those men aren't heroes."

"They are to me," the old man shouted, and some of the other folk called agreement.

"I heard they killed a notorious thief in Horbury," someone said.

"And dealt with a witch in Nostell," another crowed. "That's the kind of undesirable that the law should be sorting out."

Now the villager with the candle, the man who'd been first to meet them there in Kirkthorpe, spoke up. "You're a bailiff," he said to John. "If what you claim is true, then you're just angry because Adam and Geoffrey are doing a better job of bringing real, dangerous criminals to justice than you are."

"'Dangerous criminals'?" Will shouted, stepping forward, face flushed with anger. "You mean the so-called witch in Nostell? A healer, who the people there love and go to for help when they're poorly? That kind of dangerous criminal? Or what about the woman in Pontefract?"

"The whore?" asked the older man with the lined face, venomously.

"A widow with a small child to feed," Scarlet retorted. "Forced to do whatever she could to take care of her son. But your *heroes* murdered her and left that little boy with no one to look after him." He spat on the ground at the old man's feet. "'Dangerous criminals'. Pfft. I'm damn sure you're no stranger to the services of whores anyway, you old prick, so don't stand there acting all high and mighty."

Some in the crowd sniggered at that, and the old man's face grew red with embarrassment, suggesting Will's accusation had been accurate.

Still, it seemed a few of the villagers would defend their compatriots, but John drew his sword and swung the tip from the man with the candle, to the old man, and finally the headman. "Adam Baxter assaulted two innocent men in Wakefield tonight, one of them a friar, and then assaulted and abducted my wife." He gestured with his left hand at Amber who raised her head to show the villagers the bruises on her neck from Adam's choking fingers. "I'm not standing here arguing any more about the rights and wrongs of mob justice. Now, get back, all of you, or I'll have to arrest you too. Or worse."

Now the people did step away, cowed by the fury of these two hard men who were clearly no strangers to violence themselves. Will nodded grimly and looked at the villager who owned the stable.

The man raised his hands wide at the unspoken question, still smiling and nodding. "You're more than welcome to borrow a couple of my horses. Fine animals they are."

"Go on, then," Will said to John and Amber. "Get saddled up and come meet me where we left the horses earlier." Without waiting for a reply he ran off, sheathing his sword as he went and, with some reluctance, John followed Amber and the villager towards the nearby stables.

The man helped them saddle two animals, one of them being the biggest in the stable to take John's great bulk, and then led them out into the street where the entire village had gathered to watch them leave.

"Remember," the stablemaster said, more seriously now. "I'm no friend to either of the men you're after, so good luck catching them. But it's snowing, the ground is slippy, and I want these horses back in good condition. No broken bones or anything, all right, bailiff?"

John called agreement and thanks, and nudged his horse into a trot, allowing the animal to get used to the icy conditions. Amber came behind, comfortable enough in the saddle despite her injured wrist.

They passed the sullen villagers and found Will already atop his horse and waiting for them at the side of Adam Baxter's house.

"It was your horse he stole, John," he said and then moved ahead, towards the main road, pointing at the snow as they went. "I've scouted a little way ahead while I waited on you. There's hoofprints going this way. Hopefully we can follow them to Baxter before the snow covers them."

By this time the sun was starting to shed a little light on the earth although even when it came fully above the horizon it would be hidden by the dense clouds. Still, it did just enough to cast shadows in their quarry's snowy tracks, allowing them to follow at a decent pace.

"First the useless turd steals my wife, and now he's gone off with my horse," John railed as they cantered through the fresh, powdery white blanket that covered the roads and fields. "He's going to be sorry when we catch him. Where the hell is he going anyway?"

"Haven't you guessed yet?" Will called over the howling wind. "He's going back to the ruined house in the marsh."

"Why?" Amber demanded, obviously unhappy to be returning to the site of her, and Tuck and Farrier's, earlier ordeal. "Why isn't he trying to escape?"

"This," Will replied, lifting a numb, red hand from the reins and holding out his palm to catch falling white flakes. "I'll bet he planned on riding hard for some other town but, when he realised how bad the storm was, he decided he'd better find shelter or he might not survive. And he at least knows where the ruined house is, and probably knows no-one will be there now."

Certain that Will was right, they relied less on following the tracks which were now being erased by the snow and allowed their horses to pick up pace, carrying them ever closer to the icy marsh that lay east of their own village of Wakefield.

Adam Baxter had managed to lay out two men and carry off a woman from the house in that marsh just a few hours ago, but this time he wouldn't be facing wide-eyed, superstitious ghost hunters.

He'd be facing Little John and Will Scarlet, two of England's most feared warriors, and a woman who'd managed to break, or at least bloody, his nose despite being unarmed.

Perhaps it would be better for the fugitive if the storm took him after all.

# CHAPTER TWENTY-ONE

The miles passed quickly although it didn't seem like it to the riders, who were not dressed for this weather. Their faces were soon red, noses streaming, fingers almost unfeeling as they gripped their horses' reins.

"I'll be glad when all this is over," John grumbled, although his words were whipped away in the wind, unheard by his companions, not that it mattered. "A blazing fire, a thick blanket, and some warmed ale. That's what I'll be looking for as soon as we get back home safely."

"Did he tell you anything while you were his prisoner?" Will called to Amber, more to keep themselves alert during the almost hypnotic snowy ride than from any real desire to converse. "What's his reason for attacking all those people?"

Amber was hunched low in the saddle, dark hair standing out in contrast against the white snow that had settled on her cloak. Her sleeves were longer than the men's, offering her hands some protection from the wind but, even so, she looked absolutely frozen and John regretted bringing her. She answered Will's question readily though, in a voice strong enough to be heard. "Aye, he wanted everyone to think he was important. He thought becoming a bailiff would bring him the respect he deserved. It's all gone to his head, though, I think he's a bit mad."

"Just a bit?"

"Well, it looks like we've come to the right place to find him," John shouted, sitting straighter as he gazed into the distance. They weren't far from the ruined house now and smoke was rising from its direction. "Someone's there, and they've lit a fire to keep warm."

"We need to be careful," Will said, slowing his mount as the others did the same. "The ice and snow'll have covered the marshes, we don't want to go stepping in a hidden pool of water." He didn't explain why such a seemingly innocuous thing might prove to be fatal in this weather; his companions were not stupid.

"What are we going to do with the horses?" Amber asked as John helped her dismount. "We can't just leave them out in the open, they'll freeze to death. There's a stable nearby, Adam keeps his horse in it, but it's not big enough to take all of ours. We'll need to find someplace else."

John and Will weren't pleased about the delay, but Amber was right, so they walked until they found a stand of trees that were close enough together and with enough evergreen foliage to provide decent shelter from the worst of the snow at least. Then they pegged them to the ground close to one another that they could share their body heat.

"It's the best we can do for now," John said. "They'll be all right. We just need to get this whole business over with as quickly as possible so we can all get warmed up. Speaking of which," he put an arm around his wife's shoulders and held her close. "How are you feeling? How's that wrist? And your head, where he kicked you?"

"I'm fine," she said resolutely. "Let's just get this done."

The bailiff took a knife from his belt and put it into her uninjured left hand. "You stay behind Will and me, but take this just in case anything happens to us."

"Don't worry," she replied with a determined look. "He won't be carrying me away again."

They moved towards the ruined house, which was little more than a dark shape through the swirling snow. Normally they'd have made efforts to go quietly, looking for cover if any was available, but in these conditions it was pointless. No one in the ruins would see them coming until they were practically within the place, although the old drawbridge being the sole route inside was something of a worry.

"Look out," Will said, reaching to haul back on John's cloak just before he stepped right into a snow-covered pool of water. The bailiff breathed out heavily and muttered his thanks as they continued on, treading as carefully as possible. In some places the long grass still stood out above the snow, giving some indication of more solid footing.

Both John and Will had learned to survive in similar conditions during their time as outlaws, and both had a terrific sense of direction so they were able to pick out a safe route through the marshes and, at last, come to the massive open doorway leading into the manor house.

"Ready?" Will asked and received nods from his companions. "Be careful," he said as he stepped onto the slippery drawbridge. "Remember the man we're here for is a murderer, and he's desperate."

"He's also nice and warm," John growled. "Which means he'll be able to hold a weapon better than us."

"We'll bloody see about that," Will said and crossed the frozen moat to step into the house itself.

Amber went across next, with John bringing up the rear. The smell of smoke had grown more intense, enticing them to come deeper into the ruins with its promise of warmth and light while also making them wary of alerting the fugitive to their presence.

Just as John reached the end of the drawbridge, his boot went straight through the wood which must have been badly rotten there. There was a damp thud, and a muffled howl of surprise from the bailiff who hastily pulled his foot free and moved ahead of Amber with his sword drawn.

Will merely gave him a look and shook his head in disgust. It was amazing how such soundless communication could impart so much information. John mouthed a suitable oath in reply.

The unfortunate accident had given them away, though, as they heard footsteps running deeper within the old house, and, from the sounds of them, they were going upstairs onto the floor above.

"We know you're here, Baxter," Will shouted, looking up at what was left of the ceiling in this entrance chamber. "You can come down here and give yourself up, or we'll come and find you. And you won't like it if I have to come looking for you, 'cos it'll only make me even angrier than I already am, you useless bastard!"

"You've no authority over me," came the distant reply as the three companions started moving again, towards the rickety flight of stairs.

"I'm a bailiff, you fool," John bawled, stepping on the first of the stairs and testing it before placing his full weight on it. "Not a pretend one like you. Now get down here or we'll have to crack your skull. There's no escape – the storm will kill you if you leave the house."

"And you'll kill me if I don't!"

Thankfully the stairs seemed to be strong enough to support their weight, although they went up them one at a time, with John going first, followed by Amber and then Will.

"We won't kill you if you give yourself up," John shouted.

"But I'll be hanged by the sheriff," Adam shouted, and his voice didn't seem to be getting further away, or closer for that matter. He must have found a place to make a stand.

"Should have brought my longbow," Will said, thinking how much easier, and safer, it would be to pick the fugitive off from across the ruins, instead of having to get up close enough to take his sword to the man. The crumbling house was as much an enemy as Adam Baxter.

"Where is he?" John murmured as Will moved warily ahead, eyes scanning this way and that, ears straining for sounds of movement. Their quarry had the advantage here, for he knew the ruins much better than they did. Knew, presumably, which floors were sturdy enough to walk on, which stairs would take a person's weight, and which passageways led to which rooms.

"John!"

Amber's warning cry came too late for the big bailiff, who felt something smash into his ribs, and he roared in pain, stumbling forward under the force of the blow.

Adam Baxter had appeared from a doorway to the right, somehow moving silently despite the loose and rotting floorboards, and he'd used his moment of surprise to strike John with his sword. He stepped forward now to press his advantage before Will could come rushing back to help his friend, but the assailant had made a grave mistake.

Despite the fact she'd smashed his nose earlier that night, Adam still didn't see Amber as a threat. She lunged forward now, driven by rage and frustration and fear for her husband and, using her left hand, pushed the long blade of her borrowed knife through their enemy's thick woollen cloak and into his flesh.

He cried out in surprise but, as he looked back to at her, John recovered his balance and kicked out with all of his considerable strength. His boot slammed into Adam's back, launching the man across the room. He landed with a cry of pain, but it was lost in the frightening sound of splintering wood as his weight proved too much for the floorboards. With a terrific crash, the whole section around Adam shattered, and he disappeared from sight, landing with an even louder thud in the room below.

Will was standing beside John now, shocked by everything that had just happened. "Are you all right?" he demanded.

John nodded, but grimaced as he touched the area where Adam's sword had struck him. "Glad I wore my mail coat tonight to come to your house," he said with obvious relief. "Stopped his blade from cutting me open. Still hurts like an absolute bastard though."

"Toughen up," Will said, smiling, happy to see his friend wasn't about to die. "You need to be more like Amber. She saved you there."

"Aye," she agreed, but without the amuscment her husband and his old friend seemed to be feeling. "But while you two are standing there chattering like washerwomen, that man is downstairs getting away."

"Getting away?" Will hooted. "You think he's running off after you stabbed him and John booted him right through the floor?" He shook his head, still laughing. "I don't think so. No one's surviving that."

To everyone's surprise, however, there came the sound of dragging footsteps beneath them, heading towards the drawbridge.

"Christ above," John said, mouth agape. "He *did* survive!"

"Come on," Will said, hurrying towards the stairs which had brought them up there. "But go carefully. No point in any of us getting hurt – Baxter might not have been killed by that fall, but he's done. He's not escaping us now. Even if he got on a horse right at the drawbridge, he's badly injured and it's still snowing."

They heeded his words and took their time, moving one by one down the stairs before John and Will led the way across the drawbridge, Amber coming just behind with the knife in her left hand still slick with Adam's blood.

"Stop running," John shouted, great voice booming out into the blizzard. "We'll help you if you just put down your weapons and let us get inside to the fire."

"You shouldn't be chasing me anyway," Adam screamed back. "We're on the same side. We both stop criminals. What makes your way right, and mine wrong? I helped you capture that murderer, William Bywater, didn't I?"

"You killed an innocent woman in Pontefract," John retorted angrily.

"That wasn't even me," came the plaintive reply. "It was Geoffrey. And it was an accident. Stupid bitch shouldn't have tried to fight him off."

"There!" Will said, pointing through the drifting white flakes. They saw the hunched figure of the fugitive moving with obvious difficulty towards a low, roofless building in the grounds at the side of the house, and gave chase.

"Get back!" Adam warned, weakly waving his sword with his right hand, while cradling that shoulder with his left hand. His teeth were bared and he looked desperate, as if driven mad by everything that had happened. "I'll kill you if you follow me."

He continued to stumble through the snow, as John, Will, and Amber came after him.

"This is insane," John said irritably. "It's freezing out here. You're going to die unless you let us help you."

"Help me?" Adam retorted. "Come and help me then!"

He stopped moving for a moment, and Will, thoroughly fed up with this chase, ran forward and swung his sword. The two blades met with a ringing clatter that was swallowed up by the snow, and Adam, screaming in fury, threw himself at Will. He grabbed hold of him and, baring his teeth like a dog, tried to bite Will's face.

Instead, he felt Scarlet's head smashing into his nose and, for the second time that night, blood flowed freely down his philtrum and across his mouth.

"I'll kill you!" Adam repeated, reeling backwards into a low, circular wall. His injured shoulder rendered him unable to arrest his momentum though, and, screaming, he disappeared from sight again.

Will made it to the wall and looked over, quickly realising what it was.

"It's a well," he said, turning to John and Amber who joined him and peered down into the narrow, brick structure which must have had a depth of at least twenty feet.

Adam Baxter lay at the bottom, eyes staring up at them but not seeing their faces for the angle his head was lying at made it quite clear the man was dead.

The three companions gazed into the well, snow falling peacefully, inexorably all around, and then Amber said, "Well, that's that then. Come on, I'm freezing, and my arm is really starting to ache. Let's get back and warm ourselves by his fire for a while before we fetch the horses."

# CHAPTER TWENTY-TWO

John's horse, which had been stolen by Adam Baxter for his flight to the ruined manor, was found the next day, miraculously safe and well in John's own stable. When it had been abandoned in the marsh the horse had, using that uncanny instinct many animals seem to have, found its way home despite the heavy snow.

The bailiff, along with Amber, had not returned straight home that night, travelling instead to Will's to make sure all was well with his family, Friar Tuck, and their prisoner, Geoffrey.

Everyone had been safe, thankfully, and glad to see one another. Apart from the captive, of course, who was taken away for safekeeping the next day and transported to Nottingham to face the sheriff's justice not long after.

The coroner, and Elmer the local bailiff, had been told everything about the affair of the fake bailiffs and their crimes, and all was well again in Yorkshire. Sheriff Henry de Faucumberg sent a letter to John thanking him, and his friends, for their part in dealing with the troublemakers. He'd also included a substantial reward but, since John, Will and Amber were quite well off, they gifted the money to the people who'd suffered at the hands of Adam Baxter and Geoffrey Comber. It had been most welcome, particularly to the new guardians of the little orphan in Pontefract, and old Beatrice in Nostell. Their generosity only added to the legends already surrounding Little John and Will Scarlet.

The body of Adam was never recovered from the well, for the bailiff and coroner had gone to see it and quietly decided between themselves to simply leave the corpse where it was. To bring it out would have been both unpleasant and dangerous, given the winter weather. And, as a wolf's head – a murderer – Adam was simply not deemed worth the hassle.

Wakefield was a bustling hive of activity on Christmas Day, with men and women cavorting about the streets in animal masks, children singing nativity carols, and, of course, some of the villagers had gathered in the alehouse after Mass, to warm themselves with a few drinks, songs, and, of course, gossip.

Farrier was there, heavily bandaged, but finally well enough to be up and about after his head injury in the ruined house. Apparently his skull wasn't as tough as Friar Tuck's, who'd mostly been his old self since the day after they'd been attacked.

"But why?" Farrier asked during a rare moment of quiet in the alehouse. "Why were they going around pretending to be bailiffs?"

Tuck had already explained everything to the rest but Farrier, having been bedbound and ill for so long, was yet to hear the full story and almost feverish with curiosity.

"Well," the friar replied, "in some strange way, they genuinely believed they were doing good work. God's work, even. You see, the two of them, Adam and Geoffrey, had always wanted to be lawmen, like John there. Arresting people and, well, acting important I suppose."

"Aye, John likes to think he's important, that's true," Will said, nodding sagely. John ignored him.

"You see what I mean though?" Tuck said to Farrier. "They weren't important in their own village, just two regular workers wishing they could be something more but with no way to realise their dreams. So they decided to simply start acting like bailiffs – or, at least, as they thought bailiffs should act."

Farrier breathed out, frowning. "But they were stealing, killing people, burning down houses…"

"They believed they were punishing criminals who deserved it. Some would even say what they were doing was right."

"More ale, lads? And ladies?" The innkeeper, Alexander, interjected, smiling, and gesturing with the two jugs in his hands. "Aye? All right then, here we are. Let me just fill that for you, Elspeth…"

Even little Blase was with them, although he'd fallen asleep during Father Myrc's sermon – on courage and forgiveness – and was still slumbering peacefully. After such a harrowing few weeks everyone in Wakefield was happy to get back to normal. Christmas Day was the perfect opportunity to spend time with friends and family, enjoying the gift of life.

Where better to do it than there, in the alehouse with one another, a roaring fire, and frost on the ground outside? Some of the holly, ivy, mistletoe, and other winter greenery used to decorate the outside of the building for the past few weeks had been carried inside the day before, as was traditional, to brighten the place up. The plants would remain there until

Twelfth Night, bringing good fortune to all inside, and protecting the occupants from mischievous forest sprites.

"*This*," said John, speaking loudly so that even those in the far corners of the room could hear him. "This here is the true 'treasure'. Friends, family, meat and ale, and a blazing fire at Christmas."

"Agreed," said Tuck as the revellers nodded and raised their drinks. "All that wandering about in the marshes looking for hidden wealth, when it was right here all along." He spread his arms and smiled broadly at his companions. "Thanks be to God."

His blessing was repeated throughout the alehouse before it grew quiet for a moment, with everyone reflecting on the hopeful words.

And then Farrier said, "It would still be nice to find that gold though, eh?" which drew loud cheers of agreement.

"But we did," said John, still beaming. "At the ruined house we found the money Adam and Geoffrey had taken from folk as 'fines'. Most of it, anyway, safely locked up in a chest. Geoffrey told Tuck they were always planning to give it to the sheriff."

"So there really was treasure hidden there all along," Farrier said wistfully. "The old legends were right. Unbelievable. What a pair of lunatics those men were."

"True," Will said, nodding in hearty agreement. "And yet there's already people in Yorkshire calling them heroes, and not just their friends in Kirkthorpe."

Suddenly the door burst open, and a middle-aged man came inside, face completely pale apart from the tip of his nose which was red from the cold.

"What's the matter, James?" demanded Alexander as he finished refilling everyone's ale mugs. "You look like you've seen a ghost."

"I have!" said the man, ignoring the groan from Will Scarlet. "Out at that cursed house in the marsh. I saw a man with no face, moaning and stumbling about in the mist. Fell into the well so he did."

"Are you sure it was a ghost?" Tuck asked, looked rather worriedly at John. "If it was a real person…Maybe someone hoping to find the legendary treasure?"

"With no face?" Will snorted.

"Oh, it was a ghost all right," James replied, nodding his head emphatically. "I was just out for a walk when I saw it."

"What is it with people going for walks in that Godforsaken marsh?" Amber asked Elspeth in a low voice and the two women laughed and reached for their newly refilled drinks.

"It'll be that lad Will Scarlet shoved into the well," someone called from the far corner of the alehouse. "Doomed to haunt the marsh for all time."

"Oh, for God's sake," Will muttered, so disgusted that he put down the sweetmeat he'd just been about to devour. "That's going to be the story from now on, isn't it? At this time every bloody year the ghost of Adam Baxter will be seen falling into that well."

"Aye, Will," Tuck replied, eyes twinkling from more than just the ale. "And every year you're going to get the blame for it. Merry Christmas, all!"

And so it was, every year from that day until this, the spectre of a doomed man haunts the marshes in Wakefield and falls into the open well where he lies, damned for all eternity.

Or, at least, until next Christmas…

# THE END

### AUTHOR'S NOTE

I really hope you enjoyed *The House in the Marsh*. I wanted to start this note by addressing something I know people will be questioning: was there a house built in the marshes in Wakefield? Well, first off, the house is my own invention so you're not going to find any evidence if you go looking. Probably. I suppose you might find something similar if you look hard enough but it's not *my* house. Those old manor houses often had a moat around them, to keep out attackers or perhaps just to look grand and imposing, but how did they fill them with water? Well, one way was to divert a river. I must admit, I never knew if this was true when I started writing the book, it just seemed like the best way to do it to me, and, when I researched a bit, I discovered that yes, castle builders did fill their moats like that. So, let's imagine this is what happened here, but the builders didn't do a great job and the newly cut river channel ended up flooding the surrounding land, making it marshy for a few decades. I point all this out because, even before the book has been published, I've had people asking me how they built a house on marshy land. It's important to try and make historical fiction believable – there can't be some magical building material, it has to be realistic. Hopefully this explanation for the house's presence seems credible to my readers.

Can a story about a ghost be 'realistic' though? Yes, everyone enjoys a good ghost story, and we all have our own thoughts on whether the supernatural is real or not. The idea for this particular book came to me after reading an article in Fortean Times magazine (issue 408), about legends surrounding a place called Camlet Moat in London. A moated fort or castle here is supposedly haunted, especially around Christmastime, by an infamous bailiff called Geoffrey de Mandeville, who abused his powers and was killed by the king's men in 1144. It was quite an exciting tale so I thought I could adapt it for this novella.

The villains being *fake* bailiffs came after I'd read stories about people pretending to be paramedics or policemen. We've all read reports of men dressing as police officers in order to fine or even abduct people, but sometimes their motives are, apparently, good. Jim Bailey, from Oak Harbor, USA, was accused of pretending to be a cop for twenty-five years! He was only found out when he stopped a man attacking a woman and told a passer-by to call the police because an officer, him, was in trouble. He ended up being arrested himself. Or Andrew Vincent from London, who was arrested for pretending to be a paramedic, going so far as to have a uniform and even own a fake ambulance. You may also have heard the term 'Stolen Valor', where people pretend to be decorated soldiers in order to impress people or gain some other benefits. These imposters have often never even served in the army, but go to events wearing uniforms and even medals to fool people into thinking they're decorated veterans. William James Clark, for example, who liked to pretend he was a Green Beret captain despite being described as "ridiculously obese". He turned up at a terrible boat accident in Oklahoma and tried to take charge. Fourteen people died at the scene, and, since one of them was a real army officer, Clark took it upon himself to break the news to the man's widow! He also told the Russian Embassy he was working with the US Military to assassinate President Vladimir Putin. It seems insane but these people actually exist.

In the middle-ages, when life for the common folk was so often a dreary, hard existence, I could well imagine a couple of young men deciding they'd pretend to be more important than they really were and getting carried away with their newfound power.

Hopefully you enjoyed this winter's tale – I certainly had fun writing it. Next, I think it'll be back to my Warrior Druid of Britain Chronicles, book 5 of which I'll aim to publish around summer 2022. Until then, have a fantastic Christmas and New Year, and thank you for reading!

Steven A. McKay
Old Kilpatrick
11 December 2021

# ALSO BY STEVEN A. McKAY

**The Forest Lord Series:**
Wolf's Head
The Wolf and the Raven
Rise of the Wolf
Blood of the Wolf

Knight of the Cross*
Friar Tuck and the Christmas Devil*
The Prisoner*
The Escape*
The Abbey of Death*
Faces of Darkness*
Sworn To God

**The Warrior Druid of Britain Chronicles**
The Druid
Song of the Centurion
The Northern Throne
The Bear of Britain
Over The Wall*


LUCIA – A Roman Slave's Tale

**Titles marked * are spin-off novellas, novelettes, or short stories.
All others are full length novels.**

Printed in Great Britain
by Amazon